The Moon, the Madness, and the Magic

Enchanted Mountain

by

E.L. March

The Moon, the Madness, and the Magic

Contact Information: info@thewildrosepress.com

Cover Art by *Diana Carlile*

The Wild Rose Press, Inc.
PO Box 708
Adams Basin, NY 14410-0708

Visit us at www.thewildrosepress.com

Publishing History
First Scarlet Rose Edition, 2019
Print ISBN 978-1-5092-3032-7
Digital ISBN 978-1-5092-3033-4

Published in the United States of America

Dedication

To all those who contributed to improving this story.

Chapter One

The red haze shifted, dropping like a veil in front of Rourke Grayland's eyes. He tried to find his way through it, to fight it back, but the woman beneath him no longer had an identity, no name he could recall. Other than the physical pleasure he anticipated as he rode her hard and fast, only the fragrance of her flesh and blood interested him.

"I'm outta here," a male voice said. "The action's getting a little too tense for my taste."

Yes, it was probably better for him to leave this time. Rourke wasn't sure what he was capable of doing anymore, and under the circumstances, given the mood he was in, he wasn't sure he wouldn't take full advantage of anyone present to relieve the needs building within him.

A rustle of clothes and the sound of a zipper punctuated Dane's words. The door slammed, and the ensuing silence was like the dark burying the light.

"Dane doesn't know what he's missing." The female beneath Rourke chuckled a deep throaty promise and dug her nails into his hips.

God, that felt good.

Rourke thought about his business partner. "Yes, he does. Dane wants you, but he's not ready to let me fuck him yet. That's all."

And Rourke wasn't ready, either. He and Dane

may have shared a fair number of women, but they'd never been interested in each other that way…before.

Things were changing. Rourke was out of control. He wasn't sure what would happen if they ended up in bed together, even with a woman between them. The men had known they weren't biologically related, all their lives. According to Dane's parents, not much was clear about Rourke's background, other than he'd been orphaned at birth.

With no more than a sniff, Rourke dismissed his immediate concern.

The woman's rich feminine scent beckoned him. Hot, slick folds welcomed his throbbing cock as he pushed into her tight, wet pussy. Finally, buried to the hilt with his groin pressed against her mound, he began to move with the desperate, ancient rhythm. Mindless animal need bolted through him as her pelvic muscles gripped like a fist, clutching his full length. He pistoned in and out until only his heavy breathing and her sighs of pleasure filled the silence. The sounds he made turned from grunts of effort into low, demanding growls as his body sought more. The beast wanted more. It wanted to give and receive pain. More friction, more burn, more flame.

The only thing Rourke wanted more than all those things was to hear his name on her lips with her cry of pleasure when she came.

Seated all the way inside her, with his cockhead so deep he was fully engaged, his balls slapped against her ass with an ever-increasing momentum. He couldn't seem to drive hard enough or fast enough to find his own satisfaction, let alone the beast's. Lately, he'd needed something besides conventional sex, even something other than rough sex, to get off. Orgasm hovered just out of reach behind a sharp, keening desire, one he couldn't quite identify. The new requirements for him to reach his climax made him shudder with concern. Danger, violence, pain.

"More, harder, faster." She echoed his very thoughts.

Not a problem.

He squeezed his eyes shut and focused on fucking. Her demands pressed him on. His own needs rose like a pot on tap to a fast boil.

Blood rushed through his body, providing the fuel for the fire raging inside him. The muscles in his thighs bunched, his ass tightened, and his biceps swelled. The painful ache in his cock urged the flames higher.

He risked opening his eyes and watched the nameless woman beneath him moan with pleasure. Moonlight seeped through the window, bathing them both in silver shadows.

Dane was right to leave. Rourke should leave, too. Run.

With the moon came the madness—the madness that had been threatening his mind and his soul for the last six months, the madness increasing day by day, night by night.

When he pulled his thick, hot length out of her tight channel and paused, she arched back, exposing the thin, tender skin of her throat.

He was lost.

His heartbeat kicked up a notch as he studied the woman's long, slender neck and the pulse beneath the surface of her pale skin. He could see it, hear it call to him. Worse than being aware of the blood coursing through her veins, the blood he could smell beneath the surface of her tender flesh, was the need to taste it, to taste her.

Alive, so alive. Blood. Warm, hot liquid. Tastier, more satisfying than the drugging liqueur he'd lapped from the folds between her thighs moments earlier. So tempting.

The voice in his mind whispered, *I thirst for her blood. I hunger for a quick, tiny taste of her flesh.*

He shook his head to clear it.

Her breasts rose and fell with each breath she took. Nipples like sweet, ripe berries beckoned to him. The dark tips puckered when he touched them with his fingers. He sucked one into his mouth and played with the other. So plump and pink, so ready to…

What? Devour?

He slid his cock slowly back inside her slick heat and enjoyed the way her pussy clenched him. His fingers dug into her hips as he angled them up so he could drive deeper than before. Holding her firmly in place, he thrust and arched, filling her completely, and then began pounding into her, flesh slapping against flesh. He thought of nothing, saw nothing but the red haze.

The sound of their desperate, driving needs echoed in the empty bedroom. The sweat poured off him as he struggled with his demon. He focused on the slide of slippery skin, hot and steamy, body against body.

Beneath the subtle scent of vanilla and flowers filling the room rose the overwhelming fragrance of aroused woman and then the irresistible bouquet of flesh and blood.

"That's the way, Rourke. Give it all to me, baby.

Fuck me harder." She smiled up at him with an admiring glance through heavily lidded eyes, enjoying her pleasure, encouraging him to work harder.

Humanity seeped through his beast's thoughts, and Rourke realized that if only the woman understood what she was asking for, she'd run screaming.

"Let go. Give it all to your little Amelia, hard and rough, just the way I like it. Yeahhh."

Amelia. Her name slammed into Rourke's head, returning his mind to a moment of sanity. How could he have forgotten his favorite attorney's name?

Usually Dane's plaything, she came to him for sex play on the wilder side. She especially loved it when both of them were willing. In the office, in the elevator, in the car. Tied up or chained down, blindfolded or spanked. In fact, he and Dane often wondered how far she'd let *rough* go. Until last month, he'd never had a problem accommodating her kinky needs, but lately, Dane had bowed out when Rourke had been having trouble holding back. Rourke couldn't gauge when to stop, and still, she'd never called out the safeword.

He didn't want her to now. Not now. It was too late.

He paused to watch her writhe beneath him and thought about biting her. So much for his moment of sanity.

Fear.

Adrenaline shot through his veins.

Afraid for her, for how far she'd take the game, part of him wanted to walk out, leave her like Dane had left her, leave his beast.

Dammit, tonight, he couldn't. The beast was too strong, the beast wanted more, and a part of him wanted to taste her, too.

Her flesh, her blood called to him, and the part of him that wanted that scared him shitless.

Damn, he'd turned into a real sick bastard this year.

She scored her nails down his back and laughed. "I said harder!"

The scent of blood, his blood, filled the room. The pain did more than make him roar. It made the beast rise, powerful, treacherous, just beneath the surface, threatening to burst free. The pain felt too good. So good, in fact, it shattered his control, freeing it all up for the animal within him.

The beast wanted blood, needed it, and craved her flesh.

When Rourke rose up and arched his back into the pain, he caught a glimpse of his reflection in the mirror over her bed. The image made his pulse race. He shouldn't have risked looking.

The reflection staring back at him was that of a stranger's. His eyes had changed shape and color. Not human. Almond-shaped pupils buried within quicksilver swirls of motion.

I'm losing my mind.

Rourke lowered his head, staring down and not really seeing the woman enveloping his cock in the grasp of her tight, hot pussy, but he heard her gasp when his eyes met hers. The sound seemed astonished, surprise tinged with fear. He could smell it on her, and the scent of her fear increased his arousal. It was as if her terror inspired his cock to grow thicker, harder, longer. And the beast within him roared with satisfaction.

Her eyes slowly closed as his cock hardened and

lengthened inside her. "Oh!" The sound of satisfaction in her voice meant pleasure overcame trepidation. "What's happening?" She practically squealed with delight. "Yes, fuck me. Fill me."

He thrust into her with several quick thrusts, and this time, she moaned, the sound clearly one of erotic pleasure.

"You feel so hard, so thick, so good." She'd already forgotten her fear for the moment.

Damn. He missed the scent of fear on her.

Her nails dug into his back again as she lifted her legs higher around his back.

Exquisite pain. The sensation barely impacted his senses. If anything, it felt almost too pleasurable. What would that, mixed with her fear, bring out of him? He had control over the pain, but the fear?

Without a word and without a thought for her comfort, he gripped her wrists and lifted them over her head, plunging deeper inside her, pumping wildly, seeking his climax. Sweat dripped from his forehead in steady drops and sluiced over their bodies as he pounded into her like a jackhammer. He couldn't hold back the beast clawing inside him, trying to escape. The ache tore his insides apart as the demon within him demanded release.

"Make me come!" she screamed. "Now."

With his free hand, he slapped her ass the way she liked it, maybe a little harder than usual—the way he liked it. "Not until I'm ready."

She shrieked and bucked beneath him, driving his cock up inside her, deeper. He felt the spasms gripping his cock, but nothing was working, not the anxiety or the modest pain or the feigned violence. He wanted to get himself past this horrendous desire. The sensation sent flames up his spine, but only more violence and real fear would bring him true satisfaction.

He felt her orgasm threaten as the walls of her pussy pulsed tightly around his burning cock. His orgasm was a weak promise. Nothing less than actual violence and real pain took him past the edge of dry ejaculation to physical orgasm, and nothing took him to that exquisite point of climax where he experienced genuine relief or satisfaction anymore.

Yes, there was something inside him fighting to get out, something bigger and scarier than he could imagine, and he was afraid to let it loose merely for a satisfying orgasm.

Hold the beast back, his rational mind warned him. The image in the mirror stared back at him, full of his own conviction, the certainty he'd overpower Rourke in the end. The beast's image merged with his, and besides his eyes, he noted a more frightening change. His beard had darkened, the shape of his jaw had extended. His incisors elongated past his lips.

Shit!

Amelia thrashed beneath him and laughed again as he growled out loud. When he glanced down at her, the smile faded from her lips. The laughter died into silence as his eyes met hers and his beast smiled.

Recognition. Fear. The inevitable consequences flashed behind her eyes when they met his this time.

Ah, the fear. He almost sighed as the scent filled the room.

Finally.

Desperation fueled his passion. He released her wrists, lifted her hips, driving back into her with one long thrust, and dropped his head to her breast, biting down hard.

This time, there was no doubt her fear was authentic. She screamed and climaxed around him as he drove deeper with his hips and nuzzled her neck and bit down a second time.

Then all he could think about was the taste of the warm, rich blood in his mouth, the sweet, coppery flavor left on his tongue. All he could feel was his cock ready to burst, and all he could hear was her scream. And she screamed and screamed and screamed as he slammed into her body over and over again. The spasms from her orgasm gripped his cock like a tight fist. Her nails kept gouging his back, his arms, and his ass, inciting his beast. The scents of his blood and hers mingled, urging him on as nothing before ever had.

She screamed once more as liquid heat pooled around him. Then she shouted out his name, and he felt the smile on his lips.

Nothing gave him greater satisfaction.

Her sweet, hot honey washed over his cock, so thick and warm and creamy. The scent of her cum mixed with the scent of their blood and drove him wilder still.

Tempting, so very tempting. The beast driving his need wanted more.

Straining, he pumped faster. The weight of his large balls usually hung loose against his groin, even when he was erect and ready to come. He was so aroused they had tightened and flattened against his scrotum, practically sucked back into his body. His cock had grown so hard he thought the building force would burst the damn thing like a pressure cooker without a relief valve.

Shit, his entire body was going to explode if he didn't come soon.

The walls of Amelia's tight pussy gripped him one more time as her after-spasms milked him, and finally, the scent of her true fear forced his orgasm.

He erupted.

Rourke surrendered to his climax and collapsed his full weight on top of her. Thick cum spurted inside the condom long after he'd stopped pumping. Panting like a runner at the end of a marathon, he felt sweat pour off his body. He licked the sweat mixed with blood off of his top lip then licked his lips clean. The taste had him shooting another load of cum into the condom.

Shit, he hoped the reservoir held. Other than him, this bitch was the last person on earth who should reproduce. She had a venomous cobra's mouth with a boa constrictor's ability to suck the life's breath from her quarry. Ask anyone in Chicago law. Amelia looked like an angel and performed like a whore, in the courtroom or in the bedroom. She was his idea of the perfect attorney and the perfect bedmate. A serpent.

But then who was he to judge? A bastard with a beast taking over his mind had no room to criticize anyone else.

"Get off." She flayed her arms and pounded him until he rolled to the side. "You damn freak! You bit me! Twice!" She slapped him.

He slapped her back, a reflex that drew blood at the corner of her mouth. A small part of his sanity returned, but not enough.

He couldn't drag back enough of his humanity yet to regret slapping her. She looked surprised and a little pleased. Especially when he bent over her and gently licked her lip clean. The taste melted into his mouth like warm chocolate, and he savored the flavor. Part of him felt sickened by his action, part of him excited by it.

He ran his tongue over his lips, rolled to his back, and noted the red blood smeared on her mouth, her neck, and her breast. He smiled all the way into his dark heart. The blood on his lips tasted rich, sweet, and he'd never forget that moment of satisfaction—the moment he'd given up the internal struggle and bitten down.

Despite the power and the pleasure in that moment, had he somehow lost the battle against the beast?

Amelia's tongue licked her bloodied lip. "What the fuck?"

He reached to touch her, but she shook him off. Her growing anger brought him slightly closer to reality.

"I'm bleeding." Amelia pulled away from him and stormed off, stomping to the bathroom and the mirror. "My face! Dammit, Rourke, this is going to leave a mark! I have to be at our board meeting in the morning."

"Get over it, Amelia. It's your own damn fault. You didn't use your safeword."

"Fuck you."

"No. I fucked you," Rourke yelled after her. "Besides, you climaxed like a whore on crack. You said you wanted something edgy, a little different, tonight."

"Different, maybe." She poked her head out of the bathroom to glare at him and disappeared behind the door again as she shouted, "I just didn't expect to play Little Red Riding Hood to your Big Bad Wolf."

The water in the shower turned on right before she frowned around the doorjamb and asked, "What's with your eyes, anyway? Did you get contacts?"

"Contacts? Oh, yeah."

Shit, he'd forgotten. Yes, his eyes. He sat up and looked into the mirror over the bed. What the fuck was going on with his eyes?

Eyes? Hell, what was going on with him in general?

He scrubbed his hands over his face and shook his head. "Hey, Amelia, sorry if I got carried away. Sorry about, you know, slapping you."

She stepped out of the bathroom, raised an eyebrow, and smiled. The red mark on her cheek, the visible blood on her lip, and the smear at her breast made his cock hard again.

"Oh, yeah, and the bite, too."

"Well, a little biting is okay, but no more slapping the face. Too hard to explain." She rubbed at the wound on her breast. "And no drawing blood next time."

Her words rang in his head. *Next time?* Hell, Rourke didn't know what was going on with him, but he figured until he found out, there'd better not be a next time with anyone.

She cocked her head in the direction of the bathroom. "Want to join me?"

"I'll pass."

She looked disappointed.

He needed a reasonable explanation for wanting to get the hell away from her, but one that would help her save face. She was a good attorney, after all.

"If I get in there with you, I'll be tempted to fuck you again, and I think I've already climaxed most of my brains out my dick. I might need to salvage some for the morning." He looked at his watch. "Actually, we'll both need them at the board meeting in three hours."

He looked around for his clothes. Spotting them across the room right next to where Amelia stood made him hesitate. She cupped her superb breasts as he approached, flashing them in his face, trying to tempt him. He risked getting that close, reaching around her to pick up his shirt on the chair beside her hip. "Tempting. Very tempting."

Her lids lowered, and so did her voice, dropping to a whispered rasp. "Except for drawing blood, you were extraordinary tonight, Rourke. Hell, I think I came six times while you were pounding into me like it was your last fuck. My pussy's dripping and my knees are weak just thinking about it."

She reached out to cup his balls, but Rourke turned from her touch and forced his voice to sound light. "Your pussy milked my dick like it was a cow's teat."

He slapped her ass good-naturedly, sending her into the bathroom on her own. After he heard her in the shower, he breathed a sigh of relief and pulled on his pants. Once he was home, he'd shower. Alone.

Tonight, something had snapped. He'd totally lost control. *Next time* he was afraid he wouldn't stop. Safeword or no. He had to get with Dane and research this. They needed answers for what was happening to him.

This wasn't the life he'd envisioned. Not what he wanted. Not the woman or the sex. Not like this.

Getting away, maybe out of town for a while, might be wise, at least until he discovered what he was.

Chapter Two

Lindsey Cameron hung back. She stood as tall as she could manage, shoulders squared, head high. Unbalanced. This felt so weird.

She'd lived in Colorado in the vicinity of Enchanted Mountain all of her twenty-nine years, but tonight seemed different. Fantasy Lodge was near the epicenter of the Lore, a magical place that eventually called to all other beings at the time of their *rising*. She was no exception.

She took a deep breath and closed her eyes to gather her nerve. Part fae, part succubus, the only part of her that had ever been much of a social creature was her wolf. She was gifted, able to shift into her wolf form from the time she was a teen. Everyone always said girls matured faster than boys, but she was even more advanced than most. Maybe it was part of her fae genes.

Now, as the succubus part of her heritage approached maturity, she faced "social" on a whole separate level. Lounge Cats was the favorite hangout for Fantasy Lodge visitors, and this particular bar epitomized not only where she was but what she was. The club welcomed all shifters and humans alike.

All the planes of existence met here where the Veil was thinnest and so explained the variety of creatures that inhabited the surrounding mountains and the foothills. As often as Lindsey had visited this side of the mountain, this time promised to be different.

Besides being a typical resort, Fantasy Lodge was an erotic, hedonistic getaway. Anything and everything sexual was acceptable. She'd never needed to come here before, but tonight, she'd be going out with her succubus rising for the first time. As the next full moon approached, her succubus fought her for control. Her goal tonight—test the water, interact with the men, see if she could maintain control over her nature.

Her real challenge would be learning to control the succubus within her, especially around the alpha males who would sense the sexual predator straining to escape.

A quick glance into the giant mirror just past the potted palms had her ready to run. Thank goodness, the hallway was empty. She turned and glanced over her shoulder at the unfamiliar image reflecting back at her in the ceiling-to-floor mirror. Her hair was a mess of uncontrolled platinum curls piled high on her head. Her legs seemed to travel up the length of her body with no end in sight. A hard tug on the short, black leather skirt accomplished nothing. The material barely covered her ass, and the five-inch stilettos made her look like three-quarters of her body was leg and the remainder boobs.

She tried shoving her cleavage back into the bodice of the tiny top with little luck. The effort sent the contents of her purse scattering to the floor, and then she tried to sidestep to the left of her rolling lip gloss. That had her wobbling. Maneuvering in the shoes could get dangerous. She tried squatting very carefully, looked up at her reflection, and caught sight of…*Oops, better not do that.*

She looked around. The hall was still empty. Footsteps echoed on the marble floor, the sound drawing closer. She kicked the purse into the plants so she could retrieve it with her backside hidden in the foliage. If the quick flash of her undies hadn't been warning enough, the cool breeze on her behind reminded her she only wore a thong.

Trying to maintain her balance as she rose, she used slow, stilted movements, aimed to appear deliberate and cautious to anyone who might venture by. She tugged once more at her skirt as two men rounded the corner and approached.

She recognized them from the pictures the Council had given her when they'd assigned her to this mission. Her heart pounded when they smiled.

There was no way the men would know her, but she hoped they didn't sense anything from the wild emotions bubbling inside her, rising so close to the surface a neophyte could read them.

At first, their interest appeared to be no more than typical male awareness as they walked past her, but then one of them paused and turned her way as if he'd recalled something. She froze in place, refusing to look up and start anything.

Keep going, she willed them.

She wasn't ready to confront her obligation to the Council yet. She turned her glamour down to a mere pilot light and didn't breathe. They kept moving toward the music, fading into the dark club, but the scent of aroused wolf lingered.

Whew, that was close.

Walking in the spindly shoes presented a problem of sorts, sitting in the skirt would be impossible, and dancing might be disastrous. Her aunt was determined to throw her to the wolves. Literally.

"Damn, Celia, you did this on purpose knowing how short this would be. Are you listening?"

No response whispered in her mind.

"I'm not even as tall as some of the other fae. This skirt wouldn't cover Rachel's…well, you know what."

With the mixed crowd gathering in the club, there appeared to be plenty of opportunities to release her inner resources. Lindsey had come to accept her place among the Lore. She just hadn't expected to face it for the first time half-dressed.

In this outfit, she'd have to be careful, very careful. The vamps would drool over her long, exposed neck. The leopards, lions, and wolves would love all her exposed flesh. The short skirt and the skintight, beacon-red, come-and-get-me tank top revealed way too much.

She rechecked herself in the mirror and groaned. The thin spaghetti straps barely held the top up against her straining breasts. Her erect nipples poked through the material. There was no way she could appear in public, let alone in a place filled with aroused, hungry males of all sorts, in this getup.

She took another backward glance and shook her head. A wild curl escaped her wound-up tresses and gave her an idea. Before the approaching full moon set this month, instinct would drive her to her first sexual experience, ready and willing or not. All males would be wildly attracted to her nature as it grew stronger with each passing night. They couldn't resist their attraction to her under normal conditions, and under the present circumstances, she'd likely get mauled.

More footsteps and loud laughing. She had to

hurry.

She unpinned her hair and let it fall like a curtain of curling, pale waves draping her shoulders. It fell over her breasts, down her back to her hips, and beyond, concealing the faery wings lying flat against her shoulder blades like a colorful tattoo.

The hair would protect her like a veil.

If her true mate didn't claim her soon... Well, she'd ascend without his help, but she'd be a danger to all other males until she garnered control over her demanding sexual nature.

For some reason, the Council believed this club and its clients with every imaginable sexual preference provided the answer to her dilemma. Yesterday, the Council confirmed the rumors Lindsey had heard over the years, the ones about the prince's return and her role in the outcome of the Lore legends. Before this moment, she hadn't been so sure they were right. Now, her physical reaction said otherwise.

Even if she hadn't recognized the men from their photos, something deep inside her would have known them from their scent.

The music blared, and the low lights inside the bar flashed to the beat. She stepped to the doorway and smiled. Her succubus rose. She liked the music, the lights, and oh, how she loved the scent of males. A plethora of alpha males, Weres, fae, demons, and shifters of all sorts, a veritable feast for her feminine wiles.

They all turned their attention in her direction when she entered the club. Lindsey pushed her succubus nature beneath her wolf and dimmed her fae glamour. Looking at the hungry expressions on the faces staring at her, she was certain one of these men would gladly volunteer to ease her needs if that became necessary. For now, she wondered if she could handle letting destiny decide her life-mate, especially after glancing around the bar and seeing all the delicious possibilities. Hell, she might technically be a virgin, but she'd always had a good imagination.

However, she didn't really have a choice if what the Council and Celia, their Seer, believed was, in fact, true.

At least she'd have variety to satisfy her here among the accepting humans and the people of the Lore. Opportunities abounded, enough so she could steal into one of their dreams later and satisfy her immediate cravings. Most of the male guests at Fantasy Lodge had to sleep *sometime*.

So many fabulous men, so many options, something to suit anyone's preference or tastes. Soon, she'd discover what her own were like.

****

Strange how the straight men kept their distance from Rourke like he was lethal or something. He threw out a couple of football comments to the dude at the bar wearing a Steelers T-shirt, just small talk, but it was no-go. Except for Dane and the bartender, not a single straight male in the place said shit to him, and every gay male made a point of mooning over him. Crazy night. He had to admit he drew the attention of several guys who dropped more than a few blatant hints about being available if he swung that way. The two hot chicks draped by his sides didn't deter them, and neither did the one with her hand on his thigh, aiming a bit higher.

He scrubbed a hand across his chin. Unfortunately for everyone, and for some reason, nothing but that blonde in the hall, the one with the short skirt and cloak of pale waves veiling her tight little ass, got it up for him. When he'd passed her, she'd had him so hard he could've pounded nails with his cock given the chance. Hell, he'd been so aroused once her scent sparked his cock to life, his mind had gone blank. Then the women and one or two of the guys here in the club had given off enough sexual pheromones to start an orgy.

Even the quiet guy, the sweet thing sitting at the table next to the bar, had started to look tempting. The male flipped back his long, brown locks as he swept his tongue over his pouty lips and parted them. His large, golden eyes flashed with renewed interest and entirely too much hope until Rourke pulled himself together and shook his head.

The three women had their hands all over him, and for a brief, desperate moment, Rourke reconsidered the blowjob they'd offered earlier, but the blonde kept walking and soon disappeared into the crowd. Rourke's body and mind shut down as suddenly as it had turned on in her presence. He stood and excused himself to go look for her, but when he turned the corner to the deck, she seemed to have disappeared into thin air.

He had to find her.

Chapter Three

Rourke turned off the shower and towel dried in front of the mirror, examining himself. Something was different. If he thought shit was weird back in Chicago, he figured that was the tip of the iceberg after last night. Weird seemed like it was just beginning.

He ran a palm across his chin. He needed another shave. Lately, he always needed a shave. Not only were his eyes constantly changing shape and color, his dress shirts were too tight to button, and his T-shirts were suddenly pulling across the chest and in the sleeves. Not to mention his thighs tested the limits of his pants. He flexed. His lean muscles bulged. Working out didn't account for putting on this much bulk, and not an ounce of it was fat. He was packing on nothing but pure muscle.

Everywhere.

He cupped his heavy balls and ran a hand up his cock, watching it engorge. He grew instantly larger. Maybe the image in his head of the fragile blonde's sensuous mouth sucking his cock had something to do with it. When his balls swelled high, tight against his body, not only did the size of his erection amaze him, he was shocked he could even get aroused so soon after jacking off in the shower. Not five minutes had passed since he'd come harder than he had in years.

Lately, he noticed he was hung better than a porn

star. His cock had always been adequate. Average. Above average. He wasn't sure. He'd never worried, never even thought about his cock size. But this new, super-sized equipment? This had him at least wondering. He was huge, enviable by any standards. He didn't need a ruler to know he'd been nowhere near this size before.

He didn't even recognize his new body. It was steeled, gunmetal hard. And his sexual stamina? He'd never had any complaints in the past. Unless all his partners had faked their orgasms, he assumed he'd never left anyone wanting.

Who was he to question his sudden good fortune? Whatever brought about this extreme virility was stronger than the claims for an extended dose of an erectile enhancer.

Rourke finished toweling off and chose to ignore his rampant hormones. Last night in the bar, he'd caught the flowery scent of the one woman he wanted to bury himself inside, and he'd been burning up and aching hard when she'd been in the room. Damn, he'd been horny as hell since he arrived, and then last night, after she disappeared, no one had appealed to him. His cock had refused to cooperate.

Even with all the available pussy at the club last night, he hadn't wanted anyone after the blonde sneaked out. He hadn't lacked offers. Availability wasn't the problem. The men had been as curious as the women, attractive and sexy and damn interested in him. Hell, almost too interested—like they'd suspected he was toting some heavy-duty equipment behind his zipper. He'd avoided the men's hands as best he could. They couldn't seem to get enough of him. In self-defense, he'd asked a few women to dance, but after a quick kiss, some body-to-body grinding, and a careless grope or two, he'd felt nothing.

Where the hell had this hard-on been last night when the brunette wanted to fuck him or when the redhead offered to blow him? Shit, he'd needed it working then, not now. His big, impressive cock had been useless and unresponsive to every advance.

None of them was the one his body was looking for.

For some reason, his hormones zeroed in on the blonde, and now, he couldn't find her. Not that he hadn't tried. A sixth sense told him what—no, *who*—his body wanted and needed, and although he knew she was close by, he couldn't get a bead on her.

Rourke went to the dresser and took out his tennis shorts. He stepped into his shorts and pushed his straining cock to the side so he could zip up without maiming himself.

As he picked out a shirt, he chuckled, thinking about a comment one of the chicks had made about having to compete against both sexes.

He bunched his shoulders, shrugged, and stretched before he pulled the shirt over his head. He fisted his hands, wringing tension from his body. His muscles wanted some action. If he didn't find what his body craved soon, lethal was where he was headed.

He picked up his tennis racket and popped a couple of balls in his pocket, all the while fighting his impulses. Shoes. He needed his shoes, and socks. He spotted them, picked them up, and walked through the door to the adjoining room.

"Dane, get up. I need to work off some tension."

Rourke sat down on the corner of the bed, all the while hating to admit his dick was leading him around by the nose.

"No doubt," Dane mumbled into his pillow before he rolled over to his back. He stretched and spread out on his bed with a moan, his morning hard-on standing at full attention. "You should have fucked the redheaded twins yourself instead of forcing me to uphold the family honor. I'm beat to hell after doing the two of them and the brunette." He lifted his head and grinned up at Rourke.

Dane rolled back to his stomach, flashing Rourke his naked ass. "Man, that brunette had one fine mouth. My cock's still throbbing."

Rourke cringed. He didn't need to think about that now, not as blood surged to his own cock. The pressure made his balls ache as his erection pushed against his shorts. "Shut up. No talking."

Shit! Not a good subject under the circumstances. "Get up and put on some clothes. I'll meet you outside in ten." He bounced a tennis ball off Dane's golden buttocks for good measure, picking up his tennis shoes and socks before he headed to the door and walked out barefoot.

"Not without caffeine," Dane shouted after him.

"I'm buying." He needed one, too. A large cup of steaming, hot coffee, and if Dane was going to be any sort of competition this morning, he better get him a double espresso.

****

Lindsey stepped from her room onto the veranda, straight into the familiar, fresh scent of mountain pine. The movements of the butterflies fluttering around the morning glory vines on the trellis matched the ones in her stomach. She'd dodged a bullet last night. There wasn't much chance she could avoid him forever. Besides, what was the point? Despite the bright sun warming the early spring morning, a shiver of expectation ran up her spine. Sooner or later, they had to deal with their destiny.

Almost in answer to her inner turmoil, the soft breeze blowing gently down the green slopes sent the forest magic to soothe her. A magnificent white unicorn appeared at the edge of the forest. In a blink, the magical creature turned into pure light and sifted onto the veranda in the form of a woman.

Lindsey gasped. "Celia! Do you have to do that?" Even though Celia was her father's younger sister, she wasn't the kind of woman one could call "aunt."

"I like a showy entrance. Always have." She hugged Lindsey and pecked her niece on the cheek. "How are you holding up, darling?"

"Well enough, under the circumstances." Her aunt's powerful magic rode on the spring air, weaving its way through Lindsey's hair and over her body, relaxing the tension from her shoulders. Finally, the spring sun beat down, warming her soul and pinking her pale skin after the long, cold winter. She let out a long sigh of relief. "Thanks."

"Surely you can find a nocturnal outlet to soothe your needs while you await your assignment."

"Celia, please. I've never done this before. And thanks to the clothes you set out for me, my assignment almost found me."

"That's a good thing, isn't it? It means he's attracted."

"He was, and so was every other breathing organism in the place." The one male capable of withstanding Lindsey's compelling seductive nature for all time was here, and it unnerved her. He'd be able to support her cravings and sustain her internal succubus as well as her sexual drive for centuries if he accepted his position. "With that getup you arranged for me to wear last night, I set off every male and female pheromone in the place. I was surprised the sprinkler system didn't go off with the heat radiating off everyone. I wasn't sure whether he was feeling me or the general lust in the air."

"Even if he rejects your mate bond, this is the perfect place to work out your frustrations."

"I hardly know anything about sex, let alone my true nature. With so little self-control and knowledge, I wouldn't risk letting loose my succubus on innocent men, not without more experience."

"The lodge is famous for attracting those looking for any and all types of sexual encounters, including the unusual, with no strings attached. You should find a willing partner with some experience to guide you."

Ha, no strings. If only it were going to be that simple. "Like that's going to be possible for me under the circumstances. If the Council's plans are successful, the strings waiting for me will be like a spider's web ready to snatch me up, weaving and trapping me as well as my prey."

"All this was part of the hand you were dealt the night you were conceived, my darling girl. We know how much fate plays in the future, but there is always the chance of a good twist."

"I know. I'm not complaining. We depend on the

return of the prince, and the Lore needs a strong leader to assure the peace. I resigned myself to this fate a long time ago."

"Your mother's fae qualities should have been immune to your alpha shifter father, but she failed to recognize his *incubi* nature, the one he inherited from his own mother. This is what has come to you as the result."

The details of her ancestry were a popular romantic tale among the Lore. Desperate and hopelessly in love, her father had claimed Lindsey's irresistible fae mother in her sleep and impregnated her, changing the fae princess and her life for all time. Once her mother had fallen in love with her incubus lover, she'd crossed the lines of the fae, and as punishment, the immortal princess couldn't return to her own world until after her child reached maturity. Lindsey had been raised right there on the far side of Enchanted Mountain, close to the Tabh'rs, the portals or doorways between all the worlds of the Lore. Because she was an innocent of mixed heritage, she was a welcome and familiar visitor in all the realms, though she avoided the Underworld for personal reasons. A demon would stir her succubus nature too soon, and she wouldn't risk it. She had a role to fulfill for all her people.

"Will you be ready to confront your nature?"

"Yes, I'm fine, but I still have so many questions. Thanks for coming."

"Uh, that's what I wanted to talk to you about." Celia looked almost uncomfortable if Lindsey could bring herself to imagine her self-absorbed aunt being capable of that emotion.

"What's wrong, Celia?"

27

"Well, I really can't stay, but I did want to at least stop by to offer my support."

"Oh, I appreciate the thought, but what about my questions? Aren't you going to teach me about sex?" Lindsey heard the shrill edge to her question.

With a dismissive wave, Celia said, "No need. Your succubus knows everything you need to know. Follow her lead."

Lindsey's succubus did a little happy dance inside her that made her nose twitch and her nipples tingle. Along with the magic, another scent suddenly registered off the Richter scale, affecting her like no other. Not just any old male pheromones, this was a familiar scent. His.

A wellspring of heat rose up in her core and spread through her body like molten lava. Her insides clenched.

"Mmm, not bad." Celia picked up on the scent, too. She turned her head first right then left, seeking the source, sniffing the air until her nose twitched.

Lindsey pointed toward the tennis courts. "I checked them out at the lounge last night. Their scent was intriguing, but not this overwhelming."

Celia touched the clear crystal stone on her bracelet, and swirling colors filled it. "The full moon nears," Celia said. "The scent seems more erotic today. It will be hard to resist."

It *was* more erotic, nearly impossible to resist. The pheromones riding the air currents overpowered her will. The scent of two males was in the air—one delicious scent combined with the even more potent, more irresistible scent Lindsey couldn't quite identify as any mere alpha male wolf. She inhaled deeply.

Ah, the scent of my alpha male.

"Aren't you the lucky one? Two to choose from?"

The alpha's scent was stronger, dominant, sexually arousing, and more enticing than any Lindsey had ever experienced. The other was a familiar, insistent scent, full of passion and promise. Chills ran up her spine, and she shivered. "I'm not sure if I'd call this luck."

"Your destiny is here and now. Time to get on with it, girl." Celia smoothed her flowered summer dress and smiled benignly at her.

The hair on Lindsey's body prickled. Liquid heat pooled low, making her damp between her thighs. She forced herself to clench her fists on the railing, to hold back and hide her physical response to her mate.

"I hate this lack of control over my body. I dread it worse than facing him and telling him who and what he is, and for your information, that's really been bothering me, too. Celia, please tell me about sex so at least I know how to control my sexual reactions."

"Psht! There'd be no fun in that. No one who fully enjoys sex maintains control. Control takes all the excitement and spontaneity out of the act. It's the succubus in you looking for control. Succubae demand sexual control because their victims have so little of their own. You'll adjust. Go with your gut instincts. Go with your wolf. She'll know how to enjoy herself."

"Are you sure? Won't I need to know how to handle my nature with this man?"

She sniffed the air, her eyes sparkled with mischief, and she grinned. "Oh, my dear, he will be totally capable of handling you. Trust in the legends, darling. The Council knows your bond mate will save us from destruction."

"But Celia—"

She kissed Lindsey on the cheek. "Well, I'm off. You know how to reach me if you need me."

Celia shifted into mist and drifted toward the mountain before Lindsey could say another word.

The magnificent white unicorn reappeared at the edge of the trees, turned, and bowed to her before disappearing into the forest.

"Right, but will you answer?" she shouted after the shifting image.

"Oh, do try to handle this yourself, Lindsey. I'm off to Scotland to save two druid lairds from the unseelie fae princess who enslaved them five hundred years ago. Poor dears. You might have a bit more compassion."

"Compassion?"

"I think the naughty fae was related somehow to your great-grandfather on your mother's side. I feel a familial responsibility to undo her damage. The poor lairds have been Pri-ya *so long, only an experienced succubus can help free them from the sexual depravity of the dark fae. So, I volunteered."*

"What about me?"

"After I free them from her spell, I'll check back with you. I do hope they'll recover without any adverse side effects."

The specific side effects to which Celia referred would mean the men giving up one sexual master for another. Celia would have to wean them off fae sex, and that might mean she'd be occupied for some time, considering there were two of them to salvage from the dark fae's charms.

Chapter Four

There was that scent again. Stronger this time. Lindsey took a deep breath, held it for a moment, and exhaled. The scent in the air made her insides quake, and her hand trembled as she brushed a stray curl off her face. The heavy pheromones in the air, the ones influencing her approaching heat, filled her, almost overwhelming her good sense. She should have anticipated her reaction, but their powerful impact was greater than she'd expected.

Only a week until Beltane, and the full moon closest to the midpoint between the spring equinox and the summer solstice approached. Things would only become more intense.

The buds on the trees warned her. Time grew short, and her new responsibilities weighed more heavily on her each day. Cupping a hand above her brows, she squinted into the bright sun and looked over the landscape to the forest beyond. *Nothing.* No sinister vibrations emanating from the forest beings—yet.

So much was at stake. So many lives depended on her fulfilling her purpose. This Beltane, her first since reaching her majority, meant she could finally take a mate if she chose. Only in her case, the choice may already have been made for her, according to the Council and the legend.

The heavy scent of the male pheromones rode the

air currents, winding around Lindsey, stimulating her glamour and drawing out her inner radiance. Her secret came dangerously close to the surface, close to being exposed. With a deep breath, she tapped down her glamour.

She should have stayed and dealt with him last night. Instead, she'd run like a coward, fleeing the club even when he'd gone looking for her later. She'd known he was the one when he walked down the hall and her body responded so strongly to his scent. She'd been overwhelmed with need. Nothing had ever affected her like he had. Her breasts swelled, her nipples tingled, and her womb wept.

For her, the club would have been too public a place for their first meeting, especially if her control had weakened. Her inner nature might have seduced him on the dance floor and sent the desire spiraling outward to the others in the club. The power of her arousal could have turned the dance floor into an orgy, and the succubus within her was unconcerned about consequences. Her inner essence didn't care that this would be her first time.

Get over it. First time or not, what difference would it make? It's not like this was going to be a love-match. Why was she romanticizing this inevitable event?

Pleasurable male laughter rumbled like distant thunder from the tennis courts below. With a sigh of resignation, she walked to the corner of her veranda for a better view and discretely watched the friendly competition while she thoughtfully considered her approach.

Where should she start? Their banter filtered

through her thoughts. She wondered how the horrible tragedy of fate had brought them all together as her gaze drank in the one called Rourke—his rugged good looks, his broad shoulders, and the way his muscles rippled beneath his skin. Everything about him fascinated her. What would it be like to touch all that power?

A warm sensation passed through her body. Her insides quivered with need.

Oh, well, even if her mind hadn't settled on her mission, apparently her body had made a decision last night. In the light of day, she could see more details to confirm how right it was. He was taller than the other, which, to her calculations, would make him about six and a half feet tall or more. His hair looked every bit as dark and long, if not longer. Both men were well tanned or had naturally dark-toned skin. She understood why they could pass for twins. From this distance, the only difference she could see in their coloring was limited to a few premature gray streaks running through Rourke's temple hair. Distinguished. The sign of a born leader.

As similar as they looked, the Council and Lindsey knew they weren't twins or even brothers. She believed they weren't aware of that fact yet. If there was a blood link between them at all, no one knew of it. Those fae who remained in the realm around these mountains knew most of the true facts regarding their beginnings. They'd been born within days of each other but not to the same mother. Nor had they been sired by the same father. Yet these two men's fates had merged thirty years ago on Beltane eve, and so it seemed now with Lindsey's.

Explaining to Rourke Grayland who and what he

was became her first task, and it was the one she dreaded the most. If the men didn't know about their past or the responsibilities that loomed before them, how did one go about explaining it? How would she tell a man who had no idea the Lore existed that several days after his birth, his mother had shifted into her animal form in order to hunt and, as a result, was accidently shot by a hunter?

Did she start, "Oh, nice to meet you, Rourke. I've heard so much about you. By the way, did you know your mother was a wolf?"

Right. What seemed like the direct approach would have any sensible man laughing in her face, especially a man who'd spent his life living in the city, insulated against magic and his own kind.

Her hair rose around her like curling rivulets of pale yellow smoke on a breeze. Something would come to her.

****

Rourke slammed the ball over the net and jogged to his towel. "Game, set, match," he announced. The sexual tension seemed to lessen in the presence of the pines. This place drew him in and soothed him. He desperately needed a peaceful place.

"You sure that wasn't out?" Dane always pushed the limits.

"In by a foot."

"Out by…" The banter died on Dane's lips.

"Was not," Rourke started to argue at Dane's hedge, but he didn't miss his brother's distraction. He immediately looked over at him. The familiar cocky smile, the one Dane thought looked sexy and he reserved for only the hottest women, quirked a corner of his mouth. Rourke considered teasing him, goading him into another argument, until he followed his brother's gaze in the direction of his interest.

The scene slowed down in Rourke's mind, playing out in slow motion. Air blew out of his lungs like he'd been gut-punched, and his insides twisted into knots at the vision drawing Dane's undaunted attention. No wonder his brother looked thunder-struck. *The blonde from last night.*

The sight of the woman standing on the veranda was enough to suck rational thought from any man's brain. Not only was she perhaps the most beautiful thing he'd ever seen, but sexuality exuded from her like heat from a bonfire.

As desirable as a *succubus.*

The unfamiliar word floated on a thought and swirled through his mind as he stared at her. He'd read about them in novels—elusive beings capable of seducing men in their sleep, fucking them mindless, and draining them of their semen and, with it, their life force. If he believed in legends, the impact she had on him fit the bill, and conversely, he found himself thinking he'd gladly succumb and die happy.

Her long, flaxen hair was almost as pale as her ivory skin. In the slight mountain breeze, the strands looked like a living, breathing life form, curling and waving, rolling and whipping like ribbons of long, blonde vines. He imagined all that hair stroking him, caressing him. The sight of her sent blood pumping to his cock. His balls grew heavy, and his erection thickened, hardening as he looked into the creature's pale azure eyes. Her gaze met his, locking, forming an instant connection with him, cutting through his defenses, and gutting him with need.

The sun flickered through the rustling leaves. *Relief.* He was relieved it was daylight. This wasn't a nightmare. No, she was more like a dream, a wet dream. With the powerful light glowing behind her eyes, she might just be one woman he'd be afraid to fall asleep beside, afraid he'd lose himself in her presence.

The thought was absurd. He shook himself free of the mental images her being there conjured, and stifling a laugh, he forced himself to look away. He was being ridiculous.

Dane's low whistle escaped, drawing her attention to him. "Wow!"

Rourke heard the one word Dane managed to utter before he turned and snapped at him. "Back off," Rourke ordered beneath his breath. His insides clenched, and his mind filled with thoughts of possession. Emotions roiled within him.

"What?" Dane turned to him, his expression surprised. "What happened to our rules?"

"Fuck the rules!" Rourke snapped his head around and pointed at Dane. "They don't apply this time."

Rourke's pulse tripped a beat when she turned to glance at his brother with sudden interest. Jealousy, anger, lust consumed him. Was she trying to make him crazy? Did she want to get Dane killed? A black haze tunneled his vision, narrowing in on the woman.

"What about sharing?"

"Shut the hell up." Rourke exhaled, grinding his teeth. "Do you have a death wish?"

Dane backed up a step, and his expression filled with disappointment and confusion. He consciously forced his face muscles to relax before he explained.

"Not this time," he said, trying to sound calm and rational. Then he shrugged, still struggling to get himself under control. He took a deep breath and then quietly added, "Not with her. Never."

Dane seemed determinedly driven as he took a step toward the veranda. "I saw her first."

"No." A feral warning. The one word said volumes, and despite his best efforts, Rourke let out the low rumble rising in his throat. The sound escaped like a threatening growl, an animal sound, hardly human.

Dane whirled around to face him. "Did you just growl at me?"

Rourke ignored his question and kept his eyes riveted on the woman, all the while uttering that cavernous sound from deep in his chest.

"Hey, okay." Dane raised both hands in submission and backed away. "Don't get so bent."

One of Dane's hands clenched a tennis ball that he looked like he'd contemplated lobbing at Rourke's head along with the tennis racket he held up in his other hand. Frowning, he took a few steps back and cast a cautious look in Rourke's direction. "What's up with you? I thought this place would be good for you."

Rourke turned aside. "It is. Stop worrying." He hated being on the receiving end of that disappointed look from his brother. The wariness in Dane's eyes hurt, but he understood why. He'd been acting like an ass lately.

"*Right*." Dane dragged out the one word as if he didn't believe him.

Who could blame him? Rourke had been restless the last few months, feeling weird and acting weirder. He let out a low, sarcastic chuckle, looked up at the woman, and shook off the last of the odd sensations. He was still hard when he turned to Dane and apologized. "Sorry, it's the stress. I haven't been myself lately."

"No shit." His brother looked relieved but still guarded.

Rourke flicked his attention back at the woman. "All I want is for my groin to stop aching. Maybe the woman watching us, the one who looks like a forest nymph and projects sex like a succubus, would like to take my cock in hand and relieve me."

A tinge of pink flushed her lovely, pale skin as if she'd heard his crude comment. Even if she hadn't heard, she didn't need to be a mind reader to know what he was thinking. His damn cock was like a circus tent pole under his tennis shorts, leaving no question about what effect she had on him.

Pure stubborn male pride made him refuse to adjust himself. Instead, he winked at her and ran his tongue over his lips. The image of her thighs spread wide for his feasting made his pulse beat stronger. How would she taste? Like honey and spice?

Her face flamed bright pink.

He let his imagination run wild, envisioning how she'd feel beneath him as he burrowed inside her. How her hot, wet channel would squeeze his cock and how she'd scream out his name as he drove deep inside her.

Her breasts rose and fell with each of her breaths, and her lips parted. She innocently mimicked his action. Her pink, little tongue darted over her full lips.

His cock jerked to attention. The tight, familiar ache gripped his balls. Getting off became an immediate priority.

"Geez, Rourke, I guess you need to get laid more

than you realized," Dane said, his voice low. He frowned at the growing evidence in Rourke's shorts.

"Some women make it more urgent than others."

The woman on the terrace tilted her head and met Rourke's eyes. Her lips parted and lifted into a promise. Rourke felt her smile reach all the way to his dick.

Dane didn't miss the exchange. "Really? Then you'd better stop grinning like the Big Bad Wolf if you plan on seducing that woman into your bed."

Rourke exhaled and then inhaled her lingering scent into his lungs. "The prospects are looking up," he said in a whisper as he adjusted himself.

"Let's go introduce ourselves. And Rourke, try to wipe that hungry look off your face."

Chapter Five

The one called Dane was the smaller—if she could call a six-foot-plus man weighing about two hundred pounds small. He was slightly leaner than Rourke but still powerfully built.

When he chased down a ball rolling in her direction, the laughter stopped. Both players glanced over at her, but Dane brushed his raven-black hair off his face and grinned unabashedly. Openly interested, he exuded a lighthearted enthusiasm Lindsey couldn't deny appealed to her. He was far less intimidating than the man to his right glaring at her with eyes flashing.

"Hey, there," Dane said, ignoring his brother's attitude. He planted his fists on his hips. His Hollywood smile was meant to dazzle. "I'm Dane Grayland." He ran his hands through his hair and tilted his head in the other man's direction, his eyes focused on her the entire time. "That's my brother, Rourke."

The naughty charmer was a hard man to resist. "Hey, yourself," she said to Dane, but she kept her attention on Rourke.

He said nothing as she stared him down until the conflict became ridiculous. He refused to be the one to break eye contact, finally forcing her to look away first. The lout chuckled at her response, thinking he'd managed to ruffle her, but she took no offense. She'd get back at him later.

"Nice to meet you both. I'm Lindsey Cameron."

The surly one finally acknowledged the introductions and, to Lindsey's chagrin, did it effortlessly.

"Nice to meet you, too, Lindsey." He was all business, with a voice as smooth as hundred-year-old brandy.

No one had to tell her that if her knees wobbled and the air felt too thin, it was a good indication she should hold onto something. Lindsey was also certain those spots dancing before her eyes were a dangerous sign, too, and didn't think twice before reaching out for the railing.

Rourke's eyes burned with fire when he asked her, sounding sexy as hell and looking it, too, "Didn't I see you in the lounge last night?"

"Maybe. I was there for a few minutes, but I left early."

She'd seen him with Dane and three women, but the power she'd sensed coming from him had sent her running like a coward.

The paranormals must have all felt the same powerful alpha aura in Rourke that had drawn her to the club and then frightened her off. The women and a few of the men had openly pursued him, but Lindsey had moved to the far end of the outside deck when she caught him sniffing for her scent. Once out of his range, she'd watched him deny them all.

He had turned once or twice in her direction, then followed her, finally forcing her to shift to avoid his notice. As an owl, she could watch and remain undetected for a while from the trees. The three female shifters had turned their attentions to Dane after

Rourke, curiously, shut them down.

Turning down those women could have been no small feat when she sensed Rourke's growing needs. Why wouldn't he take advantage of their offers when sex was what people came to this place for?

In the end, the redheaded twins, two wily fox-shifters, hadn't minded sharing Dane with the brunette she-wolf once they realized Rourke wasn't going to play. They'd all appeared satisfied with the final arrangements.

She wondered why she'd continued to watch from her position in the tree outside the picture window even after Rourke left the club. In her heart, maybe she knew she didn't want to risk him finding her yet.

Dane's need wasn't quite the same as his brother's, but it called out to a part of her nevertheless. This was an unexpected complication. The man oozed charisma. He gave Rourke a cocky glance, and she noticed a flash of doubt wash over Rourke's expression. What could a man like him be worried about? Whatever it was, Dane seemed to be the cause when he said something about her that she couldn't quite make out.

A glimpse of her glamour would have a devastating effect on any male. Humans like Dane were slightly more susceptible. To teach him a little lesson in humility, she flipped her hair back over her shoulder and inhaled, knowing the impact her charms would have on him. Still, she let the heat rise in her and enjoyed the low moan of appreciation Dane released as she returned her gaze and attention to Rourke.

A low sound resembling a snarl rumbled again from Rourke's chest, this time an unmistakable warning.

Rourke was all hard angles, broad shoulders, and darkness, inside and out. She wondered if he ever suffered from the *calling*, the intuitive need paranormal beings felt to find their origins or their mates.

His brow furrowed, and his eyes narrowed, never leaving hers as he warily took her measure. He was feeling her, the irresistible attraction, but he wasn't liking his reaction.

Mine. Her succubus claimed him.

"Great," she noted beneath her breath. He was jealous, responsive, reluctant, and pissed, all because her essence *called* to him and his answered.

She smelled Dane's reaction to her glamour grow more intense and realized, too late, so had Rourke's. He let out a true growl.

Alpha. Impressive.

Shut up. Lindsey had enough problems at the moment without her inner being interfering. She ran a palm across her forehead, feeling Rourke's probing mind touch hers. Damn, the man was already using abilities she hadn't been aware he had and ones he didn't know he had, either. He probably attributed them to good insight.

Little did he know.

The responsibility of telling the men about their past was the bigger challenge, and it had fallen to her. How would she explain the Lore and the rest? Her mind mulled over all the possibilities.

How would she tell them Rourke had abilities they'd only seen before in scary movies? She could hardly hear herself casually saying, *Oh, by the way, Rourke, your brother isn't your biological brother, and you are a shape-shifter about to change for the first time.*

What? What are you?

Oh, sorry, not sure what you'll turn into on Beltane, because no one can be sure who sired you. But guess what? You're meant to lead the people of the Lore.

That almost seemed easier than the rest. Telling the men about their dark history might well be her task, but convincing them of the real truth might be harder still. She dreaded telling Rourke that the man he believed was his father all his life wasn't. How did one broach a subject that delicate?

She looked into the Rourke's suspicious gaze. He knew she was hiding something. She forced her eyes shut to hold him at bay for a moment.

Would unraveling the truth tear the men's relationship apart?

Did any of this matter to the outcome of the legend?

She doubted it. When it came to fate, Lindsey was sure that beings were nothing but pawns, a means to fulfill the end.

Sadly, what didn't matter to fate she was certain mattered to the two men staring expectantly up at her.

Her pulse raced. The man who would have to accept her as his mate glared up at her, barely masking his wary curiosity. He knew something was up. Her heart ached as she wondered what the future held for Rourke.

Unfortunately, fate never gave anyone choices.

All fears aside, when Rourke discovered what his surrogate father had done, Lindsey prayed he didn't kill the messenger.

In defense against the open animosity she read on his face, she allowed all her virtues to climb to the surface. The hell with playing fair. She'd use the arsenal at her disposal.

Not human.

The Council told her that he was part human and male enough to recognize her assets. *"Rise up and show yourself."*

He was less affected by her glamour than Dane had been, but affected he was nonetheless. Her succubus was very talented for a novice. What Lindsey didn't see affect him, she felt. That other connection he fought, the unerring mate bond between them, was too strong to deny. She recognized the pull in the air and yet knew he'd resent it.

She resented wanting him, too. The emotions she felt confused her.

He wouldn't fall easily into destiny's trap. *Good for him.* She didn't want him to be easy.

She drew on her power. What kind of fae succubus couldn't affect a part-human male?

He squared his shoulders as his eyes locked with hers, looking slightly confused but stoic in his stance against her.

Transfixed on his face, her gaze melted into his and mixed feelings swirled within her, almost overwhelming her. He was hard and commanding, and she wasn't sure she would bend to his will. She had been a powerful force unto herself until now and was bound to grow stronger. Yet she couldn't bear to think he'd approach their union as if he'd been compelled to it.

Lonely. Empty. Needing. Wanting.

I know. He's here now. She sympathized with her inner soul, and yet her emotions were embroiled, good sense with lust. She didn't fully understand why, but she resented his resistance to her.

Finally. It was about time he returned to take his rightful place. Damn well time he claimed her.

Perhaps she gave away too much. Perhaps she revealed her inner feelings in her expression.

His jaw clenched, and she knew she'd been right. Great, he was already defensive, and she still had to convince him that his destiny was bound to hers, no matter what their own thoughts were on the subject.

After watching his heated expression grow cold staring her down, she began to believe persuading Rourke to leave the corporate world behind would be far easier than convincing him to accept her as his mate.

Not you. Us. And him, her succubus clarified.

Him? Dane? A ménage? Hmm, maybe there is hope.

Then the beast's heated, silver haze flickered in Rourke's brown eyes for a moment, supporting the Council's theory and sending a frisson of concern through Lindsey. Once he started to experience his first shift, especially now with his impending change, he'd take her just because the beast within him demanded it. That didn't mean he had to like it or her.

Even she felt the pull of the Beltane magic here and now in the bright light of day. The time of the full moon drew closer.

She tilted her head, angling a soft, understanding smile at him, hoping to ease the strain of this first encounter. Rourke Grayland, fifth-generation shifter, was heir to the greatest seat of power over the lightest and darkest elemental beings of the known worlds, all the Others of the Lore, and Lindsey was his balance, his destined mate.

I am for you, Rourke Grayland.

****

Until a few minutes ago, when he'd seen the blonde watching him, he hadn't known he could be this attracted to anyone. The pull from her on every level was so strong it frightened him. After being wound too tight for so long, he could sure use an unconventional release. One without the worry of the cost to either parties. For some reason, this didn't feel like it came without consequences.

His hands fisted at his side, garnering control.

After not being able to find the blonde last night, Rourke had sulked while Dane had taken full advantage of the local benefits. Now, he could certainly think of a few hundred needs he wanted to fulfill with this woman. Where had she gone? Who had Lindsey been with while he'd looked for her in the lounge and on the deck?

Unwarranted jealousy needled him. He reluctantly admitted, if only to himself, as strange as it seemed, he'd somehow sensed her presence, even though only briefly last night. Something about her seemed familiar to him when they'd made eye contact.

"Maybe I'll see you later," she said.

Then she turned and waved good-bye, and Rourke's heart lurched in his chest, wounded, as if he'd lost something or someone. He shook his head, trying to toss off the weird emotions he experienced as she went back inside her suite.

When he finally stopped staring at the door, he

noticed Dane looking at him like he had two heads. He wiped the sweat off his brow with his forearm before he admitted, "I need a shower. A cold one."

The breeze swirled around him, and curiously, instead of losing control, he gathered it to him. Almost as quickly as his aggression peaked, it drained out of him. The anger and the pointed jealousy affecting him dwindled as the scent of grassy meadows mixed with the unique fragrance of the woman. Then a different awareness touched him. An incredible sensation stirred. Something he would never admit or consciously identify—a trace of enchantment—filled him. All his hostility calmed, dissolving on the breeze.

Peace may have replaced the hostility, but then he recalled the throbbing ache in his cock. Nothing replaced the lust.

"You'd better shave. All that bristle is going to leave a rash on the tender skin between her thighs. That would be a shame, a real shame." Dane sounded wistful. "Are you sure you don't want to sha—"

"Don't go there. We were having enough problems with that the last time."

"Touching your cock was an accident, dammit."

"Fine. Then forget it. I'm just not ready to go there again right now." Rourke tossed his racket to the side. *Shave?* He ran a hand over his chin. He'd already shaved this morning. The muscles in his shoulders tightened when he felt the day's growth after only two hours.

Guess he needed a new razor. He shrugged, trying unsuccessfully to loosen up. "The hell with the cold shower. I think I'll go get out a few kinks in the hot tub." Maybe the circulation would relax some of the tension out of his muscles and relieve the concerns jackhammering in his head.

Rourke walked back to his room, thinking over what had brought him here. Nights filled with strange images, terrifying nightmares, blood. He wasn't sleeping well. His appetite was off.

Off? Uh, not off. It was more like downright bizarre.

And his appetites had changed in everything from food to sex. His sexual preferences had always leaned towards sex on the controlling end of rough. Without any doubt, he had strong dominant tendencies. Lately, he was coming up with more and more controlling ideas. To make matters worse, suddenly, the normal boundaries of dating and sex had become too stifling for his needs.

His new inclinations bordered on being downright creepy. He'd wanted to bite the hot marketing VP while he'd been plowing into her from behind two weeks ago. He'd gone so far as to nip her before she'd told him to lay off the tooth action.

During the next ménage encounter, Dane had seemed different. Since he'd brushed against Rourke's cock, some wild inner beast in Rourke wanted to make him submit, make Dane take Rourke's cock down his throat, and then he'd seen Dane's gaze actually fall on his cock with interest. Rourke had slapped the thoughts down, and Dane had been right to leave. He should run now, because Rourke wouldn't be happy until he had everyone on their knees.

He'd changed so much over the last month that he didn't recognize himself. There was the incident last week with his attorney. She was pretty kinky, but in the middle of the evening, even Dane had sensed Rourke's growing fierce penchant for rough sex and left them to their own devices.

Rourke had bitten her. Twice. Not that she hadn't deserved it after practically tearing his back apart with her nails. What had really freaked him out was that he swore he could hear every thought in her head at the board meeting the next morning.

Spending so much time and energy contemplating how he was losing his mind pissed him off. At least he'd always been able to depend on his sanity, even when nothing else made sense. Like his background or the DNA results he and Dane had gotten back a few months ago.

Recently, the intensity of his mood swings extended beyond his sexual aggression. He'd become edgier, more vicious in his business dealings and less patient. He'd always prided himself in the rational control he utilized in business dealings, and now, he couldn't afford to lose that edge. Holding back his emotions lately, both in bed and in the boardroom, nearly bordered on the impossible.

With his sexual needs escalating to more and more aggressive levels, he worried that too many women in his circle might talk. Some were already uncomfortable with his fierce sexual intensity. Hell, he was uncomfortable with it himself.

Where would it stop?

At first, he'd ignored what was happening to him, then his wild inclinations made him wonder how far he'd go. Where were his limits? If he didn't find an outlet to safely discharge some of his pent-up frustrations soon, he figured he'd explode. God help anyone around him when that happened, because he didn't have any idea where he'd draw the line. Not anymore.

He'd been sick and disgusted with himself the day he'd passed the travel agency and glanced inside. He wanted answers, and he had to get this craving out of his system. The answers had hummed in his head like a swarm of bees buzzing around, drawing him into the store.

The travel brochure about Fantasy Lodge had practically jumped into Rourke's hand. A vacation. The marketing for the lodge couldn't have been clearer. Rumors claimed every self-gratifying need could be fulfilled there, and according to the plagiarized theme, *What happened in Arctic, Colorado, stayed in...* He sighed with relief. Just what he needed. Time off and a safe place with willing partners.

When he'd brought home the brochure and mentioned the idea of a vacation to Dane, his brother thought an early birthday getaway sounded like a great idea. The photos in the brochure confirmed the place was exactly what they needed. He carefully read aloud the part spelling out how the place provided enough hedonistic promises to satisfy a horny college football team.

Dane, being Dane, wasted no time making the arrangements for them to take off work and then called and made the reservations for both of them. Just thinking about all the possibilities had made Rourke's groin knot with expectation.

He'd taken another look at the brochure and sensed something familiar about the place.

Or had it been something else?

The hell with waiting. Rourke was a driven man when he decided to go look for Lindsey. He may have warned Dane off, but he recognized the turmoil conflicting with his brother's better judgment. He was tempted to cross the line this time, to break their solemn pledge, and Rourke noted that the woman wasn't immune to his brother's charms, either. Rourke hadn't missed how she had reacted to Dane. Rourke had to stake his claim before Dane did.

Chapter Six

Last night, like now, Lindsey felt the need to run from Rourke. Yet in the light of day, after she'd turned away from him, she had to force herself not to look back at either man. A frightening urge washed over her, and fear gripped her to the core. The sudden realization that Dane needed her, too, had been too staggering to contemplate with Rourke staring holes through her.

Lindsey turned and went inside, not actually surprised to see the visitor dressed in robes of white in her kitchen, rummaging through her spice rack. "Celia, what happened to Scotland?"

"I need coriander. Don't you have a properly stocked spice rack?"

"Celia? Scotland?"

"The *Keltars* are handling it now, and anything else can wait. They've been imprisoned in fae this long, a few days more can't hurt."

Her aunt had dismissed her assignment to return. Things here must be serious. Lindsey decided to express her concern. "What if we're mistaken? Maybe he is the wrong choice for leader."

Celia waited no more than a heartbeat before she responded. "No, I've seen it in the written prophecies. He *is* the future chosen leader of the Lore."

"And Dane? What of Dane?"

Celia stopped searching the cabinets and turned,

wide-eyed. "What of Dane?"

"Oh, nothing. I just wondered what it is about him that…"

"That what?"

"Maybe he's just a very strong-minded human, but I think he's Other, too. Though I'm not sure why he's lagging behind. I thought he was older than Rourke."

"Perhaps not. No one knows for sure. Maybe he's the one. They are so alike." Celia remained cautious with her responses.

Lindsey didn't miss her wily ways. "Not really." She flopped on her bed. "I don't think my biggest problem will be persuading Rourke to take on his role as leader. He is exceedingly alpha, alpha enough to lead not only the pack but the entire Lore, but what I think the real problem will be is he won't want me."

"I know you've sensed his power," Celia said, "and so have all the Others when he's around. As Council Seer, I can assure you I am not mistaken about your bond mate. And, Lindsey, he wants you already."

"Really *me*? Or me, the succubus?"

"I believe he wants you, but you must remember you are both. Only one with a trace of succubus can control an alpha strong enough to be Lore leader. That leaves just you available."

"These two men are notorious for their philandering ways. Neither brother is a likely candidate for a life-mate, Celia, let alone a bond-mate."

"Situations change. People change."

"Fine, if you say so. I can probably learn to accept his sexual affairs. If he insists on an open relationship, I can live with that. But the mating could change him. The bond could force monogamy on us both. Then what? He'll hate me."

"Ah, yes. It might. He might."

He'd accept the challenge of leading. He always had. Her challenge would be convincing him to accept her as his mate, unless he decided it all on his own.

"Rourke's reputation with women has painted him as a scoundrel of sorts, bringing along his charming brother as his naughty sidekick. He won't take kindly to having destiny decide his fate," Celia said. "Somehow, you'll have to make him think it's his idea."

"I know. I suspect he never liked being told *what* to do, and now, he isn't very likely to agree, in my case, on *who* to do."

"Hmm. Surely, that would be difficult for one of his nature, but is that your true concern?"

"No. I've seen something different in him. Something I've never seen, something dark. Maybe unseelie, maybe something else. Could there be another beast inside him?"

"Hmm, another. Really? Unseelie? Maybe." The crooked smile on Celia's face seemed strange. She didn't sound as surprised as Lindsey thought she should be at her announcement. "Well, my darling, use what resources are at hand." Celia turned to Lindsey and smiled benignly then disappeared without even a poof.

"Bitch! What resources?" Lindsey jumped off the bed. "That's easy for you to say and poof outta here. What kind of aunt leaves her favorite niece when the going gets tough?"

Lindsey actually stamped her feet.

"I hear you." Celia's light laughter faded away. *"You are all my favorites. Try less subtlety."*

Less subtlety. What did that mean? Her aunt was

useless, but "less subtle" was the equivalent of "more obvious," wasn't it?

Aggression might be a helpful tactic to use on Rourke. She didn't have much time to skirt the issues, not if she was going to aid the new regent through his transition and hers. There was no time left for niceties.

Maybe Dane would understand and assist her when the crucial time came. As a geneticist, he could make a life's study of this place. She knew she could convince *him* to stay. He liked her. Rourke was a different story. Once he discovered how he'd been deceived all his life, there would be no accounting for his reaction.

Chapter Seven

Subtlety? Had she seriously entertained the thought that being *less* assertive would work with Rourke? A virgin wasn't exactly the sexually aggressive sort of woman he was used to. With someone like him, she might need even more than her glamour to get his full attention. Nothing less than *blatant* sexuality and her sensual succubus was going to work against a sharp mind like his.

Lindsey paused outside her door, dropped her towel on the chair, and stepped into the hot tub adjoining her private garden. With a strong, magical, mental push, she invited him, all the while knowing he would have to come.

The pull between destined mates was alleged to be irresistible. It had already influenced her feelings. She prayed to the goddess it would be the same for him.

Earlier, leaving and closing the door behind her was one of the most difficult things she'd ever done. What should have been an easy turning away had been nearly impossible. With the scent of his distinct, masculine fragrance drawing her to him and the magic driving her urges to mate, she'd had to impose her sheer will against them. Once the door had blocked his scent, the horrible ache spreading through her soul eased to a hollow, empty feeling in the pit of her stomach.

The *longing*, that need between mates to bond, to

be together always, stirred her basic instincts to go to him. She was already feeling the consequences of separation, and they'd barely even spoken. But the *voice* affected her, too, that ability mates had to sound-imprint to each other's voices. He hadn't said much, but he'd turned her insides to mush. She wondered how much stronger this mate bond would get between them after they actually touched? Or more?

The sudden image of their bodies wrapped around each other in a naked embrace caught her off guard. Her insides quaked with the effect. The *vision.* The ability to create a link between destined mates existed so that they could endure minor separations. The problem was that it was so real, the mates actually physically experienced the sensations and emotions of the experience.

She closed her eyes and leaned her head back, letting the gift of vision sensually fill her mind. The skill linked all the senses between them, as if they were actually participating in the actions. She could see through his mind and he through hers.

The tiny air bubbles from the jets tickled her flesh, building the tension rising within her as her desire for him increased. Her body wanted him as much as his would want hers. Neither could deny this attraction between their inner beasts, no matter their human desires or choices.

A heated flush moved over her skin like the rising tide over a sandy beach. She sensed his presence before she barely opened her eyes and saw him. He'd come. Followed her here. Tracked her like a wolf would his mate.

Exhaling a long, slow breath, Lindsey enjoyed a

brief moment to study him beneath her lowered lids. His thighs were eye level, and so was the impressive bulge beneath his bathing suit. He was a magnificent male specimen, no matter the species. She risked lifting her gaze to follow the trail of dark hair up to the thatch covering his thickly muscled chest. Not too much, just enough hair to soften the hard planes of all that bulk. His pulse beat a strong tattoo at the base of his throat. The urge to lick him there and feed had her running her tongue across her lips. The pulse beat picked up.

His jaw clenched. She inhaled and let her eyes study his lips. God, he smelled delicious. Her mouth watered just thinking about kissing him, having those hard lips plundering hers. Her tongue swept the corner of her mouth, and she heard a low warning rumble. She dared to meet his eyes.

As she anxiously waited for him to say something or do something more, his wary contemplation worried her.

"I thought I saw you last night." His pointed stare trapped hers. "You knew I had to come." The words sounded like an accusation as much as a fierce refusal to succumb. Although hearing him admit his need filled her with hope.

"I wondered if you felt the urges, too." Her words were like a breathless whisper. "After the way a glance from you made me feel last night, I hoped…" She didn't want to elaborate since her own motives weren't clear.

"It was you I saw, then? I saw someone, felt an inexplicable attraction to her, but she disappeared. I searched, but you hid." His blatant accusation challenged her.

"I stayed in the shadows, but I think you sensed me."

"You. Yes. I felt like I was looking for... How did you do that? Some new kind of perfume?"

"I didn't do anything." Her glamour shimmered, catching his attention.

The pulse at the juncture to his throat picked up a beat. He turned away and looked around. She followed his gaze, certain he was evaluating their privacy. The isolated deck was empty except for the two of them. He turned and stalked the area, fixated on the lock, and swiftly secured the gate.

Lindsey didn't miss the birthmark on his upper back. The dragon. *My God, what does this mean?* "I guess we aren't sharing the hot tub with anyone else." Good, they'd be alone.

"Nope, I don't think so." With the gate locked and the vine-covered trellis providing sufficient privacy from curious onlookers, he seemed satisfied to continue their conversation where she'd left off.

He turned those golden eyes back to her. "You may not have done anything, but there's something about you. Just now, I started to go to the hot tub across the complex looking for you, but something directed me here instead. *You did that.* How is that possible?"

There was that hint of accusation in his tone again, as if she had a choice in all this. Anger with her predicament niggled at her. "I don't understand the dynamics, but I'm drawn to you, too."

She couldn't tear her eyes from his or stop her body's response to him any more than he could to hers. And damn it, the more she listened to his deep voice and that low pitch, the more the scent of her arousal increased. As her desire intensified, becoming even more obvious to him, it drew him to her as much as his scent locked her to him. The attraction was a circular trap, entwining them tighter with each passing moment.

Thank goodness they were alone, because despite his quiet presence, she knew just how much her scent affected him. The evidence of his erection strained even harder inside his bathing trunks.

The heat burned her cheeks, and she shuddered when his eyes narrowed on her nipples. She didn't have to look to know they were poking obviously against her thin, white bathing suit top. From his glare, he wasn't happy with his reaction to her.

She squared her shoulders and raised her chin defiantly, daring him to accuse her of something else. But instead of the sarcastic words she was coming to expect, Rourke allowed a slow, sensuous smile to take over his expression before he gave her the full wolfish grin.

Now, he did look remarkably like the wolf she thought he was.

"Good." He brushed the back of his hand over her pebbled nipple. "For a minute there, I thought I was the only one feeling like this. It's good to know I'm not alone."

"Would it make a difference if I told you I don't always respond to my body's demands?" She couldn't resist goading him.

"No." He sniffed the air. "Not at the moment."

"Just no?" She expected the man to be arrogant. On one hand, it pissed her off just a little. On the other, arrogance seemed downright sexy on him. "Not now?"

"Well, part of me is relieved to know you're

discriminating…"

Her breasts ached for his touch, and her nipples tingled, waiting for more. "And…the other part?" She bit her lower lip, refusing to look at the *other* part.

He stepped into the tub and paused, his cock at her eye level, so long and thick she couldn't miss the outline of his crown detailed through the material. "Guess."

"Oh, I s-see."

Rourke didn't move, but his cock twitched beneath his shorts as he hardened further. She studied his erection and realized she had to force her eyes away from the tempting bulge.

Her gaze rose, slowly, reluctantly. "You believe I can be persuaded?" Her gaze stopped at his neck. She dared not look at his eyes this time. Instead, maybe it was a mistake. She took in every detail of his broad shoulders. Next, her attention sank lower to his amazing chest. The thick muscles there were beautifully defined. She wanted to trace her fingers over them, to touch his tight male nipples, puckering under her scrutiny, tightly beaded and aroused. The dark hair sprinkling his chest trailed down his abdomen, slipping beneath the bathing suit he wore and pointed straight to the huge bulge. Yes, she wanted to touch him there, too. She inhaled.

"Good, then you get my intention." He ran a hand across his tight abs and lowered them until he stopped the downward path and moved it to his hip.

Arrogant bastard. She bit her lower lip to keep from moaning. "Hard to miss." *Oh, God, no pun intended.*

He chuckled and cupped his balls. "Tell me I haven't misunderstood yours."

She ran her tongue over her lips and swallowed hard. Her mouth was so dry she did it again. What would touching him feel like? What would tasting him be like? His cock jerked under her scrutiny.

She was too distracted by her own imagination to see his reaction to her until he touched her face.

"Answer me. Have I misread you?" He tilted her chin up and looked deep into her eyes as if searching there for answers to all his questions.

Not realizing she'd been holding her breath, she exhaled. Her voice sounded different, raspy, when she finally answered. "No."

He tilted his head. His gaze dropped to her mouth, and he brushed his thumb across her lower lip, forcing her to part her lips slightly. "Good."

The temperature in the hot tub suddenly felt as if it soared ten degrees, melting her from the inside out. Her pussy clenched. Her inner core anxiously wept the fluid heat, readying her feminine folds for him. Oh, how she needed his lips on hers, his mouth and hands roaming over her skin, exploring her body.

He leaned down and licked her lower lip, nipped at it, and brushed his lips over hers as if he'd read her mind. "I don't know why I'm so desperate to be inside you, but I feel like I'll die if I don't get to bury myself in your hot, wet core."

He pulled her up and out of the water, drawing her body against his. The feel of his silken skin over steeled muscle tantalized her as he ground her along his raging erection.

The sound he made, low, deep, and sexual, was one of pleasure and pain, reminding her of a delight she'd never known. She wanted to be naked, needed the skin-to-skin contact, longed for his caress, and desperately wanted his hard length intimately pressed to her mound. When he accommodated her last wish, she sighed, resigned to her mission. This act might be worth the pain of a broken heart should he reject her.

More hot fluid seeped between her thighs, preparing her body to accept him as they sank into the water, his big body looming over hers.

"I want to taste every inch of you, eat your pussy until you scream my name." His words made her hungry.

Oh, yes. She wanted that, too. She closed her eyes and leaned her head back, exposing her neck. He kissed his way down to her shoulder and cupped her breast with his hand, teasing her nipple through the thin material. He wrenched the top of her bathing suit down, exposing her nipple to the air, and then he bent in to lick, nibble, and suck.

Oh, yes, this pleasure may be worth any pain.

Any pain until one thought shattered her. The mate bond shouldn't be like this, forcing their attraction. If only they had the time to grow to trust one another before the bond took over, tying them to each other for eternity. At least she knew what to expect when this was over. To their detriment, she could sense he approached this seduction like every other sexual encounter he'd ever had. Unfortunately, his attitude for now was "fuck her and forget her."

He has a lot to learn.

She jumped when his hand pushed her thighs apart, his fingers exploring the tender skin between her legs. *Apparently so do I.*

"Oh, my goodness, that feels so wonderful."

"Wait until you feel this, then." Pushing the string of her bathing suit aside, he freed her pussy lips to his exploration. The sound of her gasp escaped although she tried to hold it back. The pleasure in her womb built as his thumb caressed her nub and one long, thick finger parted her cleft. She tensed.

"Relax." He groaned in her ear when he cupped her. "Damn, your clit is so swollen I want to suck it. Would you like me to do that?" He rubbed her engorged nub and pinched it slightly. "Does this feel good?"

Sparks shot through her body. Lindsey moaned. "Yes." Then she melted into his hand and couldn't do anything except nod.

For an instant, she wondered who the true succubus was. He was stealing her life force with every touch.

Chapter Eight

Rourke waited for emotional distance to settle over him, the one he experienced with all women, even the ones he bedded. Not this time. Not with this one. Now, when he needed to distance himself, why did he feel so damn in tune to Lindsey?

After last night, when no one else in the whole damn lodge had held his interest, he felt this, now. This desperation.

He couldn't wait to fuck her, yet he intended to take his time, lots of time. He wanted to spend hours with his face buried between her legs, licking and tongue-fucking her until she came in his mouth, screaming his name over and over again.

Rourke felt a ripple of amusement. Dane was right. He did have a god complex. He loved to hear the woman he was fucking cry out his name as she came. He narrowed his eyes and focused on her mouth. He couldn't wait to hear his name on her lips as she climaxed. Then he'd devour every drop of that dense fluid seeping from her core.

Sure, she was just another woman—albeit an extraordinary woman—but he had to keep reminding himself this was just another fuck. Wasn't it? *Fuck her and forget her.*

He stared into her eyes. *Just another fuck.*

Something shifted inside his chest, and it didn't

feel like the beast this time. *Forget her.*

Right. Then why did he crave inhaling her scent more than he needed oxygen?

Because it was her damn fragrance that kept him rational in a world gone insane.

He wanted her mouth on his cock and her blood in his veins.

Whew! Did he say rational? Maybe not quite. He was getting carried away.

Take a minute.

He pulled away, examined her soft, pale skin, her raspberried nipples, and her fragile, narrow wrists. He should tell her what he was like. He should warn her what being with him would mean to her safety.

Rourke lifted the tiny pieces of her bathing suit top back into place. Breathing harder than he could ever remember doing from a simple make-out session, he nuzzled her ear. With his rough edges buffered for a second, he whispered, "If we do this, you need to know I get rough, really rough."

****

Lindsey leaned into the warm breath against her neck. With her eyes closed, enjoying the feel of his coarse beard rubbing against her, lightly abrading her skin, she barely registered his warning. The warning was unclear, and his lips felt too good kissing her neck to have her caring.

She asked anyway. "Rough, like punching me, slapping me around?"

"No. Hell, no." He pulled back and stared at her. "Nothing like that."

"Oh, okay."

A wry smile tripped over his lips. "Maybe a little

spanking now and then, but nothing violent like bruising. Unless you're easily marked?"

The hard-ass had a dimple. Her insides melted. "No, not so easily. But maybe you should be more specific." Lindsey didn't know what else to say. She didn't want him to stop, so instead, she said nothing more. She wanted to kiss that dimple and slide her lips to his mouth, but she didn't move, waiting for him to explain what rough meant to him.

Wolves had fangs and bit. She expected rough.

When he spoke again, his hands traced a path down her shoulders, and his voice sounded thick with arousal. "I like my sex hard and fast—well, not all that fast." As he reached her wrist, he stroked her pulse, suddenly more gentle than the tough guy image he'd portrayed all along. "You are so delicate, so very—" He stopped touching her.

"Don't stop." She cut him off quickly before he changed his mind. "I'm much sturdier than I look. I want this, Rourke. Don't try to scare me off or bail on me now."

"Make sure this is *how* you want it."

He was warning her, giving her this one chance to bolt.

"I think I can handle anything *you* like."

"You're a spitfire, aren't you?" He chuckled. "Don't be so sure about the anything part."

"If you like it, I'm sure it has to be good." Taking his hand, she picked up her towel as she climbed out of the hot tub to lead him to her room. "Come." She didn't miss the crooked grin he sent her.

****

Come? Damn straight! Rourke had every intention

of doing just that, multiple times. Even if his attachment to her made his mind wary, his cock would follow her into hell right now if she asked. For all he knew, between the demon in his head and the damn divining rod in his shorts, that's exactly where he was headed.

The water beaded on her skin and glowed with radiant light. "Which room?" he asked.

"That one, with the door ajar."

He needed her too much to wait. "Good, then I can do this." He scooped her up in his arms, noting she weighed practically nothing as he carried her inside the room and kicked the door shut behind him. Only pausing long enough to locate the bed, he realized all the rooms were set up the same.

Thank God, her bed was exactly where his was, because that was as far as his cock's patience would let him go. The thing had a mind of its own and kept straining beneath his trunks to get out and touch her ass.

Rourke practically threw her on the bed and stood over her like a guard. "Take off your top. Slowly." His demand resounded in the room.

While she untied the strings to her bathing suit with painfully slow intent, he never took his eyes from hers. Instead, he pushed down his trunks, springing his cock from the pressure of the material, and let out a sigh of relief.

He hadn't thought about what he was doing until her eyes dropped to his groin and opened wide. When he glanced down, he winced. He looked back up at her, carefully watching the expression on her face. He could almost read her calculating mind evaluating his length and girth. There was no doubt about what bothered her when her hands flew to her breasts, pressing the tiny white swatches of material back over her nipples like a shield.

Her reaction had him grinning. Unfortunately, he couldn't suppress the chuckle that escaped as he tried to reassure her. "Don't be concerned. It'll fit. You'll see."

Her gaze flashed to his. *Liar* was what he read in her expression.

His patience with the ache in his balls reached the end of the line. "Your breasts—I want to see them again."

He stepped closer to the bed and studied her reaction. Apprehension froze her in place when he reached over to pull the string from her hands. The material slowly slipped past her fingers, exposing more skin than she could cover with her small hands.

"Don't be shy. I've already tasted those berried tips." He gently removed her hands from her breasts and placed them over her head. "Don't move."

Rourke dropped his gaze to her hips. "I can't wait to taste more."

He switched his attention to the small piece of material attempting to cover her bottom. The triangular swatch wouldn't be much of a challenge, no barrier at all, but it was blocking his view. Totally focused on his one goal, he slid his hands slowly up her thighs to the ties at her hips. As he pulled the side ties with slow, painful care and excruciating patience, he wondered why. For a man used to taking neither, he was suddenly enjoying seducing her with his slow, deliberate assault.

He slid the material off her body like he was unwrapping a precious gift. "Yes, perfect." Her pale blonde curls were trimmed into a tiny patch at her mound. "There'll be no going back now or changing your mind. I can't wait to see your pussy. Is it wet for me?"

He spread her legs wide with his hands, baring her pussy to him, and stepped back, staring his fill. "It is. Bare, naked, wet, and pink." With appreciation in his tone, he marveled. "You're beautiful. Lovelier than anything I've ever imagined. In just a minute, I'm going to bury my face between these thighs and lick you." He tangled a finger through her curls and then pressed it to her exposed, swollen clit. "Here."

She shuddered beneath his hand with arousal he could feel vibrating in the air. He wanted to fuck her, bury his cock in her and fuck her until he couldn't think, couldn't feel, couldn't breathe. But the other side of his nature wanted to take his time and enjoy each touch, each sensation, each moment of delight. God, this was agony.

Going slow. *Unbearable.*

Soft caresses. *Hell.*

Admiring the creature waiting for him to pleasure her. *Pure heaven.*

Her folds separated like a flower, opening beneath plump, petaled lips, soft and moist with dew. "I can't wait to kiss them, taste them. I want to see if these lips feel like your mouth."

When he separated her slit, thick, hot nectar poured from her, making her channel slippery, just the way he liked. Her pussy was beautiful and perfect, and her scent called to him.

Lindsey inhaled, took in a deep breath and held it while he pressed one finger inside her virgin-tight opening. He was testing her readiness. But when he met her gaze, something behind her eyes flashed, telling him there was more to all this.

He stilled. Suddenly, she appeared too childlike, too innocent.

Even though she gave off sexual vibes like nothing he'd ever experienced before, there was innocent dread stamped on her face, and it made him wonder why. For a moment, he hated that he'd turned her desire to panic. Now, when he looked at her, all he saw was a frightened animal cowering on the bed, not the seductress from the hot tub.

He gave her some space, wondering where that seductress had gone as he absently touched her breast, lightly circling her nipple. She arced off the bed, pressing into his hand. Her body demanded more.

Still here. But there was something else.

He sniffed the air. Fear. *Oh, damn. No.*

The scent of her desire mixed with the scent of her fear. The beast inside him roared. The combination had his inner demons fighting what was left of his civilized side.

He licked his fingers and separated her folds, pressing one finger inside her. He slid it slowly in. She was wet, more than dripping wet. Her juices leaked like honey pouring from an overturned jug. She moaned at his touch. There was no doubt she wanted him, even though her opening clenched and tensed, trying to prevent the invasion of his single finger.

He whispered, "Relax." Maybe his size did intimidate her.

Taking his time, he spread her cream over her clit then into her opening and probed deeper, with two fingers this time. She jumped back. He held her in place and explored. *What the fu-u—?* He bumped up against an unfamiliar obstacle and froze.

Whoa. His cock twitched. *Virgin.* The beast roared. *Mine!*

Surprise smacked him in the head. When he'd seen the strange expression on her face, he'd suspected her of something. This had never crossed his mind.

He'd never had one, never done a virgin. Hell, he didn't know if he could, certainly not without hurting her. His demon cheered.

He tapped the monster back, ashamed.

When he touched the barrier of her virginity again, assuring himself he hadn't been mistaken, he heard a more solemn voice in his mind shout, *Mine.*

He pulled out his finger. Shaking his head, he stared at her soft, pink folds in wonder.

"Don't stop. I have condoms," she insisted. Her voice held a hint of panic. "I'm prepared."

More fear. Her desperation stirred the beast in him. Was she afraid because he'd stopped or afraid because he wouldn't?

Damn him. He didn't care. He had to have her. The decision was already made for him. His body refused to walk away from this woman. He rolled off her legs, lay back against the headboard with his arms propped behind his head, and growled. "Get the condoms," he ordered.

Her terror drove him to the brink, to a place where he wouldn't be able to stop. But fuck him, he'd hold the damn beast back if it took everything he had. Something about her made him want to guarantee she enjoyed her first ride.

As she shuffled naked to her bag, only a hint of

self-consciousness showed. *Might as well take the opportunity to admire the view.* The two cute dimples at the top of each rounded cheek tempted him to go after her. Her long hair covered her back.

To hell with waiting. To hell with patience. He wanted to kiss her delectable ass.

A happy thought made him grin. He wanted to bite it, too. *No biting this time.*

She took another step, and then her legs distracted him. His gaze slowly drifted down those dancer's legs. Later, he planned on wrapping her long, limber legs over his shoulders so he could lap up her liquid fire. She'd be too far gone to worry about the size of his cock or the prickle of pain when he breached her barrier. There was no way to avoid the inevitable pain, not completely. But all the pleasure he had in mind would distract her. Then he'd take hours making her forget the twinge of pain as he initiated her into the sexual world.

Her hair swung across her back from side to side as she walked and exposed the large, colorful, life-size tattoo of fairy wings on her back. It was beautiful, almost mesmerizing. He was going to kiss every spot on those wings when she came back to bed.

Chapter Nine

The economy box of condoms said *large*. But after seeing him erect, Lindsey wondered if they came in a size called wow or gigantic. Surely, these wouldn't fit over that, that… Surely, *that* wouldn't fit inside her.

Yes, it will.

They were fated for each other.

She could almost hear Celia's melodious voice saying, "*You will suit.*"

With a shrug, she pushed back her hair. Rolling her shoulders, she braced for the inevitable and walked back to the bed. The condoms didn't really matter to her or to him. These were only for pretense. She couldn't get pregnant now, couldn't get human diseases, and even if he didn't know it yet, neither could he. He was as immune to human illnesses as she was.

Still, she wished she had more experience with all this sex stuff or with males in general. What kind of succubus didn't know about sex? She looked at the box in her hand in wonder. Would he expect her to know how to put one of these on him? Once, in a movie she'd seen, a woman place the condom in her mouth and roll it over the male with her tongue.

What if she accidently inhaled?

Oh, no. And there was so much of Rourke to cover. He'd be a lot to handle with only her tongue and lips.

"What's that worried look on your face?"

She couldn't stop herself. She glanced at his groin and sighed. "Nothing."

He chuckled. "Trust me, it's not *nothing*."

"I—I didn't mean it that way."

His eyes lit up, and a corner of his mouth turned up. "I know." He beckoned her and patted the bed next to his hip. "Come over here."

When she sat back on the bed, the smug look on his face dispelled some of her nerves. His erection rode high on his abdomen, and their sexual pheromones filled the room.

"Come closer, right here."

She lifted her chin. "I guess I have to trust you, then."

He nodded. "I see you brought the *whole* box."

When she sank down on the bed, she shrugged like a petulant child. He drew her body under him as he took the box out of her hand and placed it on the nightstand. His face assumed a comical, teasing leer. "Thanks for the compliment."

"What compliment?"

"Thirty-six times? You either think I'm superhuman or plan on killing me."

"I wasn't s-sure—"

"No sweat." He kissed her hard with plenty of tongue and moved his lips over her jaw to her ear. "We'll see just how much you can take and see what kind of damage we can do to that box. Sound like a plan?"

****

The aroused scent pouring from him put her more at ease. From the size of his erection, at least she knew he was pleased with her body. Her gaze caressed every inch of him. She'd imagined what it would be like to touch him all over. Now, she'd get her chance. His dark, tightly beaded nipples stood out on his expansive chest. She wondered if he'd enjoy having her handle them, lick them, or suck them as he had hers.

Maybe she'd go with her instincts. A succubus's instincts should be dependable. *Shouldn't they?*

Rourke interrupted her thoughts. "I can see you're thinking too much."

She cupped his face in her hands. "Yes, I am. Thank you for being so understanding."

He started to jerk away. She figured he was unused to the intimacy, but at the last moment, he stopped and kissed the tip of her nose. Instead of reacting like she'd expected, he stared at her and sounded amazed. "You're giving me, a virtual stranger, your virginity, a valuable commodity you've held on to for, what, twenty-something years?"

She glanced aside. "Twenty-nine, almost thirty," she said and nodded.

"Hey, darling, I'm flattered." His eyes narrowed. "But why are you thanking me?" He angled her face toward his, making sure she made eye contact with him. When she didn't answer, he continued, "It'll be my pleasure to take what you offer with no strings attached." His grip on her chin tightened. "Right? No strings? There'll be no hearts and flowers on my part when this is over. You understand, got it?"

His hands felt like a vise squeezing her face, and his words felt like a vise constricting her heart.

"I know. I don't expect you to feel anything—"

He stopped her words and warned her. "But you

know *you* will."

She grimaced when he gripped her chin even harder, demanding her undivided attention. Cold emptiness replaced the heat in his eyes, and distance settled over his expression. "You *will* feel something."

"Will I?" The emotional see-saw effect was beginning to aggravate her, and her voice cracked. "You must think pretty highly of yourself."

He cocked his head to one side and gave her a crooked grin. Without telling her to "get real," his know-it-all expression spelled out in no uncertain terms what he thought of her. *Naive fool.*

"It's not about me, but trust me, you will remember and feel something for me, guar-an-teed."

"Why? How can you be so sure?"

His voice was almost a whisper when he finally answered her question. "Darlin', you never forget your first."

She gasped. "Oh! Right." With an attitude she dragged out of the depths of her alternate nature, she winked at him. "Then you better make it very good."

To better make his point, he blew on her nipple lightly. She was tempted to arch into him, but before she could respond, he bent his head over her breast, and the warm, moist heat of his tongue followed the warm air, satisfying her for the moment like nothing ever had. She groaned, and a reaction sparked from her nipple to her clit.

He licked her nipple, sucking it deep into his mouth while he weighed her other breast in his hand. The draw on her breast from his mouth sent a flood of moisture seeping from her pussy. He lightly pinched the tip of her other nipple between his fingers. The sensation forced a lightning bolt of pleasure to drive somewhere even deeper inside her.

God, she wanted every pleasure he could offer.

Cupping his head to hold him in place, she demanded more of these mind-blowing sensations, wanting it to never stop. When his mouth left her nipple, the heated absence left her feeling cold, open, naked. He stared at her nipple with longing in his expression while his warm breath teased at her wet skin. His lids lowered sensually, and the heated look on his face made her want to satisfy his every desire.

He played with a strand of her hair, circling her areola with the loose curl that had fallen across her breast. He teased her nipple with the curl for a moment before he rose up, kneeing her thighs apart, and covered her body with his. The weight of his long, heavy body on top of her, his cock pressing hard against her clit, made her want to weep with gratitude.

He dragged his hands through her hair, forcing her head back. His hard eyes bored into hers as he took her mouth with his, tonguing her deep until she could barely catch her breath.

When he released his tight hold on her, his stiff smile gentled, and his hands loosened in her hair.

Lindsey purred back, forcing herself to sound self-possessed, something she'd never been. An urge washed over her. She needed to touch him, wanted to know what his cock felt like in her hand. Curiosity compelled her hands to start the slow exploration down his body.

He stilled, expelling a low groan when she cupped his balls and ran her hand up the long length of his shaft. His raised eyebrow showed he'd been surprised by her brazen move. "I guess I had better make it memorable."

"You will," she said with lowered eyes. Then she looked up and added, "I have complete faith in you."

His grin surprised her. He gave her a real, honest-to-goodness, mind-blowing, "I've-seen-the-light" smile. Lindsey suddenly felt privileged to be the object of that smile. A man who could smile like that could get anything he wanted. His face lit up, looking so beautiful in a stark, masculine way that in that one moment, she would never have forgotten him, not if she'd had a hundred men before him and thousands after. There was this strange bond between them that made her want to please him, bring him around, and draw out that special smile more often.

"Let's go over the rules."

"Oh! There are rules?"

Rourke chuckled. "Yes, just a few." He gently wrenched her hands over her head. "Number one, no more touching me before you come."

"But I w-want to touch—"

"Number two, no arguing. I'm in charge." He raised his brows in question. "Unless you think you know what you're doing? Do you?"

She lowered her eyes and shook her head slowly.

"Then trust me. Number three, pick a word, any word. It'll be your safeword. If you want me to stop anything, no matter what or when, I will. Just say the word. Make it short, so you can get it out fast."

That made Lindsey think twice about where they were headed. "Uh, red?"

"'Red' is a good safeword. I've used it before."

"You?"

"Not me, my partners. They chose it."

"Ah, do you do this often?" She felt strange asking these questions while lying naked under him. Naked and at his mercy. Especially after she realized the quick twinge of jealousy didn't help.

"It's how I am. I'm dominant, aggressive. If I don't have hard sex, I don't come. And, darling, I plan on coming inside you plenty."

Her heart stuttered in her chest, with excitement, not anxiety. She'd never had sex, and she didn't know if she'd like this level of dangerous sex, but a thrill sang through her system just the same.

"Don't worry, I'll take it easy this first time, at least until we get past this first obstacle. Then we'll take it from there. You decide what you like and how far we go, then we don't turn back."

Wait until he found out how far they'd have to go. She felt like a traitor. He was trying to take such good care of her, and she…well, she knew where they were headed, and it spelled out a whole lot of pain for him.

What choice did she have? For that matter, what choice would he have? They were both trapped by who and what they were and duty.

"You just lie back and let me get you ready. I'm going to eat your sweet pussy until you beg for mercy. What's the magic word?"

"Uh, r-red?"

"Don't stutter, it'll take me longer to stop."

Stop? Why would she want him to stop? She'd never had her skin tingle or her insides heat like she'd been branded. He'd sucked her nipples until they were bright pink and sensitive. Only his hands or his mouth or his big body satisfied her ache to be touched. When he'd spread her legs apart and admired her, she'd squirmed, partly with embarrassment, partly with a need she couldn't quite identify. He'd already trained her body to respond to his hands. She suspected his mouth would be even better. "Why would I want you to stop?"

The laugh sounded like it came straight from his heart. "That's my girl."

Without warning, he pressed his head between her legs and lapped at her juices. His tongue drove into her and sent her heart flying. His lips kissed her, and his mouth devoured her with the enthusiasm of a starving man placed before a banquet table. Her body wanted him to eat his fill. She could barely breathe as he brought her to the edge of desperation and pulled back over and over again.

Anytime now, her body felt as if she could jump off a cliff and fly if she could just get enough leverage to reach the right soaring altitude.

His fingers strummed at her clit like a maestro, and his tongue lapped at her cleft while she begged him for more when she could catch her breath. "Rourke, I need, I *need…*"

"Tell me, baby, what do you need? Do you want me to stop? Use the magic word—"

"No! Don't stop, ever."

He chuckled again.

Lindsey was on fire, ready to burst into flames and explode. She couldn't allow him to stop now, not when she was so close to… "I think I need you inside me."

"Not yet, darlin'. I don't want to hurt you. Can you take two fingers?"

He pressed two thick fingers inside her and

scissored them. She bucked against his hand. "Yes, more."

"Easy, take it easy."

"More. I need more."

"How about this?" He pinched her nipple lightly as he increased the speed and pressure on her clit with his thumb.

Hot, liquid fire poured from her pussy as the spasms clenched his fingers inside her. "Yes, oh, yes!"

Lindsey screamed as a thousand stars burst behind her eyes and the convulsions rippled through her.

Rourke quickly rose between her thighs. Lifting her knees, he opened her folds with his fingers first, lubing his cock and her entrance with her cum. While her orgasm wracked her with spasms of pleasure, he probed deep with his fingers until she felt a quick burn and a stinging pop inside her. His mouth sucked hot at her breast and nibbled on her nipple, driving the thundering desire within her.

He broke through her hymen while pleasure mixed with the brief moment of pain until only satisfaction remained. If she could form a rational thought, she would have realized what a wily devil Rourke was to devise such a pleasurable experience for her first time. How he managed to initiate her into the world of sexual pleasure he enjoyed. The pleasure and the pain. But maybe she'd think about all that later. For now, his hands and mouth were creating all kinds of responses from her body.

He kept stroking her clit as he settled his cock at her entrance, and then she felt his thick, mushroomed head trying to press inside her. He squeezed his full length into her, one slow inch at a time. The stretching and burning eased as he filled her, conquered her.

The conflicting sensations confused her. Her clit wanted more pressure, demanded more speed, but her pussy felt invaded, violated, and, at the same time, filled, needy, and desperate. Without understanding what or why, she wanted something else. She started a rocking rhythm with her hips.

He picked up the pace with the ancient beat as she propelled herself against him. Surrounding him inside the circle of her arms, she melted into his passionate, open-mouthed kiss. All the while, his tongue fucked her mouth and his cock plunged past her broken barrier, driving deeper and deeper, his powerful hips pumping harder and faster, until he touched her womb and forced a guttural moan from her.

She imagined what it would be like to take his cock in her mouth and taste him, drive him to this same sort of crazed need. She wanted to suck the juices from his balls and swallow his cum when he reached orgasm. She could almost feel him in her mouth, almost taste him on her tongue. "Mmm."

Still, she craved more of his deep, thrusting strokes inside her. Her body joined the beat as he plunged in and out of her, filling her completely. The friction of his groin rubbing against her clit as he fucked her had other sensations compelling her body to move against his.

She should have been self-conscious, letting her inhibitions go like this, but she had to come with him inside her for the link between them to be effective. Tingling sparks traveled up and down her spine. The heat inside her core burned like a furnace. The effect spiraled higher and higher then plummeted until she felt like she'd fallen off a cliff.

She screamed his name with her release, and he growled above her, all masculine power and dominance as he thrust in and out, each stroke more demanding than the last, more powerful, more desperate. But his inability to unleash the burden within him hurt her. She had to help him let go, to free what was inside him.

The faery dust from her climax settled on her skin, mixing with her perspiration, turning it to light, shimmering silver and golden dew. She touched a finger laden with the crystal magic to his lips. He nipped her finger, threw back his head, and roared. The long muscles in his neck strained as he thrust. His cock lurched inside her, and he came like mighty thunder. The air sizzled, and the ground shook.

Then the mate bond between them started weaving its magical threads. They curled through her body and grew denser minute by minute.

Dammit, he'd been right. She had emotionally connected to him as soon as his cock entered her body and slid past her broken barrier. But this? This was more. He was going to be upset when he discovered what they'd just done.

They both exhaled and collapsed in a heap on the bed. She was too exhausted to worry about the consequences now. Besides, she felt too good to ruin the moment with worry. Reality would rear up and poke her soon enough. For now, Rourke stayed wrapped around her, buried deep. She felt fulfilled for the first time in her life, but they were both too spent to think.

With his fingers tangled in her hair, he groaned in her ear. "Sorry. Your orgasm forced mine in its wake. I would have liked to have held out longer for you. The aftershocks inside your pussy are still gripping my cock, extracting every last drop of cum from me. Useful little talent, that."

"I don't want this to end." She wanted more of him, all of him secreted within her, body and soul.

"Greedy little thing." He took a few deep breaths and regulated his breathing. His low, rumbled chuckle vibrated through her. "Don't worry, we're not done by a long shot. As long as you keep that magical pussy of yours contracting around my dick like this, I might stay hard forever."

Lindsey tried to relax and slow her breathing while he embraced her. The minute he'd slid into her virginal channel, she'd known there was more to all this than the damn legends, more to him and their instinctive attraction than she'd comprehended.

He was something other than what she'd been told and much more than what she'd expected on every level.

Wow, had she thought he had a lot to learn? Maybe they all did. Maybe no one fully understood what was about to happen this Beltane.

If the Council hadn't told her how potent Rourke could be, perhaps they didn't know. She wondered how she'd missed all his abilities when she'd probed his mind earlier. Perhaps he was mutating even now.

He'd somehow instinctively learned to block over the years, and his abilities were already the most powerful she'd encountered in the Lore. Who would guess he was still developing?

As far as the Lore was concerned, he was basically an infant. After this experience, she asked herself, an infant *what*? What was he?

That was the question she should pose to Celia. For

some odd reason, she didn't think Celia knew. She might suspect something about his past, but Lindsey didn't think the Council or Celia had all the information on Rourke and Dane. One thing Lindsey was sure about was that Rourke was more than a mere wolf-shifter.

She caressed his face and drank in his male beauty, studying his expression. He lifted his weight and shifted to her side. She felt empty without him inside her already. But the expression on his face looked more relaxed than she'd ever seen him. He leaned in and let his breath fan over her lips before he touched his to hers. His hair draped over her breasts, entwining with hers, binding of its own accord. She opened to him.

She hadn't expected to feel so emotionally overwhelmed by the sheer act of surrendering to him.

And why not? Hadn't she bestowed her innocence into his hands like a virgin bride on her wedding night?

Why not?

For crying out loud, she was part fae. She should be above such petty feelings. If not the fae part, then surely the succubus part should be handling all this differently. She was the one who was supposed to emotionally drain the souls from her lovers, and yet the power of experiencing a part of his body buried deep inside hers and the rest of him surrounding her protectively made her want to weep with total satisfaction.

He'd warned her she'd feel like this, have this attachment to him. Not specifically to him, but this commitment to the man who was her first lover. Maybe he was right, but she suspected the real truth was that this union would trap him, too. Whether he wanted to care for her or not, he was doomed.

Suddenly, she realized she felt tied, linked forever to the man in her arms, the one who had brought her sexual pleasure for the first time, just as he'd promised.

"Hey, stop thinking." He rolled over on top of her, kissed her senseless, and angled her hips higher. He was already hard again. He repositioned himself and moved back inside her, burrowing deeper with his huge cock. "Put your legs over my shoulders."

Thrusting with a brutal pace, he hammered his rigid cock faster, slapping his hips against her bottom with his balls smacking her ass. His breathing turned to short, shallow gasps as he pumped.

He rose up on his knees, stretching her body out, and looked at all of her. He parted her cleft, pinched her clit, and rubbed, not missing a beat with his hips and quickening his pace. The sound of skin slapping against skin aroused Lindsey again to a fevered pitch.

The succubus in her gave off the intoxicating scent, drugging Rourke's human nature and slowly freeing his beast. Her skin prickled in his presence. The beast inside him enhanced his stamina, giving him the kind of strength he'd need to sustain her.

Show yourself. Who are you? The succubus wanted his beast.

Lindsey experienced the rising tide of heat, the raging passion building within her again. She wanted his hands all over her, his mouth kissing every inch of her flesh, and his eyes devouring her with that look of admiration she'd seen on his face earlier.

She sensed the internal glow of her glamour rising with his cock burrowing ever deeper inside her and his fierce, driving strokes urging her to completion.

Her essence wanted to merge with his. Everything

she was, everything she could be, wanted him body and soul. It was the *binding*, and there wasn't anything she could do to stop it. Nor did she want to.

When he turned his head to kiss the inside of the leg she had thrown over his shoulder, his expression softened. Behind the rugged mask he wore like armor, elements of the part of him she hadn't noticed before broke through, exposing his tender side, the side that she clearly recognized needed love and compassion. The side she longed to be part of.

Without conscious thought, her hair started to caress him. The living strands were part of her succubus nature, deriving and giving pleasure like any other appendage.

"God, you're so beautiful you're glowing. Your hair, it's amazing." He sniffed a strand as it wrapped around his shoulder.

He was behaving like a caring, tender mate instead of the distant, aggressive dark lover. She feared she was going to become so emotionally entrenched in his tenderness that she would lose herself in him.

They were in so much trouble if the Council was wrong. Because once they bonded, they wouldn't be able to be separate. Things were happening too fast. She needed more answers.

This is so not good.

Her hair reached for him like her heart wanted to. She was becoming seduced by his powerful alpha male side and consumed by his beast. Better not to let herself be swayed by his human side as well.

She released more of the pheromones, the ones that would bring on his beast and push back his humanity, and then held her breath, waiting.

His eyes turned from gold to black. They angled up and changed shape, from round to oval. The dark shadow of his beard thickened. The sinewy power of honed muscles rippled beneath her touch, and it was all she could do to hold back her orgasm.

For some reason, she found herself compelled to speak. "You are for me." Lindsey let the words fall past her lips, powerless to stop them or the compulsion to bind him to her.

"Oh, hell, yes. *I am for you*, baby, and you are for me."

Her heart lurched when he returned her words. His promise uttered in his deep bass voice brought on the signals of her climax.

Her internal spasms rose like a series of waves inside her.

"My skin is too tight." She whimpered, holding on to him. "Something is happening to me. Can you feel it?"

Rourke pressed his lips to her ear and murmured a warning. His voice sounded different, raspier, lower than usual, when he growled out, "Don't come."

She felt ready to burst. "I have to come, I need—"

"Not yet." He slid his cock out of her entrance, leaving her empty, aching, and wanting.

The tingling in her pussy made her want to mount him and ride his cock like he was a stallion.

As if he'd read her mind, the wolf reared its head behind his human eyes. *Ah, yes. Wolf.* She'd always known there was wolf in him.

"Turn over. Get on your knees." Rourke growled, his lack of patience obvious when he flipped her over, positioning her on her hands and knees. He spread her thighs, bent down, and licked her, clit to ass. Then with a roar, he drove his thick cock back into her, reestablishing the simultaneous beat of their hearts.

One of his hands held her in place around her waist, and the other caressed her, breasts to mound. She was so preoccupied with the pleasure of his touch she hardly noticed that the hand at her waist looked almost iridescent, shimmering like colorful, beaded scales.

She wanted to focus, but the volcanic, heated pressure rising inside her was ready to explode.

The low growl in his chest grew louder when he lowered his mouth to her neck. The soft brush of his lips conflicted with the bruising force of his cock thrusting inside her. Then surprise—his teeth scraped the tender skin on her neck, and she realized he was going to bite her. Mark her.

She squirmed uselessly beneath him, trying to turn, to stop him. The urge was instinctive; he didn't understand what he was doing or the consequences. He held her in place.

The power inside him surged, and his teeth elongated into fangs and punctured her jugular. The sensation of him siphoning her blood brought on her climax. Unable to prevent the pleasure riding her as he sucked at her throat, she came in an explosion of light and sizzling, electric shocks shooting through her system. The faery dust drifted around them like a sandstorm. The spontaneous waves of her orgasm gripped his cock. He plunged deep within her until he could go no farther, emptying his seed into her as he drained the blood from her neck.

Tiny dots danced across the black veil behind her vision. She had to stop him or die. "R-red," she whispered.

He stopped sucking, pulling his mouth from her vein, and collapsed on top of her. He pushed her slightly to the side, but he didn't withdraw his cock. She felt the tremor of his orgasm still seizing within her. "I love being inside you, babe."

Well, he'd marked her with his words and with his teeth and then, finally, well and good with his seed. He was going to be really pissed off when he realized what he'd done and that he'd come inside her twice without a condom.

He'd bound her to him. This time, totally bound her. By words, seed, blood, and deed. Rourke's essence filled her and bound them ever tighter. Even though she hadn't fully bound him to her by blood yet, they were connected. Something else besides her blood-taking was missing in their bond, though.

Strangely enough, she sensed the answer was close by. The missing piece to their puzzle was a being. Not human. Someone or something of the Lore hovered just barely out of her reach. Wolf. He called to her. A void, an empty longing, drew her to the aching soul like a bee to honey.

Rourke had called to her that same way, and now this other soul ached with hopeless, jealous pain. She'd been meant for Rourke, but she'd wondered about her connection to Dane. What did it mean?

She didn't understand.

Chapter Ten

Dane closed his eyes and waited outside her room in the enclosed private garden. He'd been in big trouble from the minute he'd caught Lindsey's scent in the air and then again from the minute he'd seen her. He was a scientist. He of all people understood imprinting, and damn if he hadn't imprinted on her. Fisting his hands at his hips, he dropped his head against the pine wall and allowed the pain to sear through him. It made him feel better about acting like a fucking voyeur listening to her and Rourke fuck.

Rourke had called her first. Claimed her. This time, Rourke was adamant about possessing and keeping this woman to himself. He'd made that damn clear.

Neither of them had ever been so set on a single woman. Hell, if they'd both wanted the same one in the past, the women had been happy to have them both. No one cared much one way or the other. The women didn't want a relationship, just the kind of great sex that he and Rourke could provide. A ménage—different approaches, different styles, different tastes—a sampling of everything.

Strange thing was, as far as Dane could remember, neither he nor Rourke had ever been serious about any of the women.

Why now, why her, and why had they both zeroed in on this one woman?

He didn't know what to do. He felt as if he were losing his mind. Rourke had taken her for himself. Not just taken, but to Dane, it seemed like a claiming. He wouldn't share the one woman Dane had to have, and he believed he had to have her or die.

Nothing like this had ever happened before. He'd never felt like this, but then, the DNA tests proved you can't believe everything you're told. Something was wrong. Something was off.

His stomach churned. The thought of never having her made him physically ill. That realization sliced his soul into irreparable pieces while he waited outside the room where he knew Rourke touched Lindsey the way he wanted to touch her, to kiss her, to bury his cock inside her and give up his soul for her.

Tense and upset, he couldn't tear himself away from their presence despite the turmoil churning through him. He felt at a loss as Rourke seduced Lindsey deeper and deeper under his control with his compelling dominance.

Standing there listening, imagining Rourke kissing her, touching her, sinking his hard cock deep into her tight, hot pussy, was pure torture, yet he couldn't move away. The guttural sounds of pleasure seeping from the room nearly drove him to distraction. While Rourke fucked the woman he ached to possess, her damn emotions and something else called to him, dragging him here to agonize through the act. The impossible link he endured with her threatened to gut him.

Dane wished he could walk away, cover his ears to the sound of sex, and erase the visions of the two riding each other to climax, not once but two, three times. With a deep breath, he tried to wipe the scene away. He ran a hand over his eyes and felt the wetness. With a pass of his arms, he wiped away the dampness with his shirt sleeve.

Even with his internal pain screaming at him, nagging him to leave, he couldn't walk away. Try as he would, he couldn't close his mind to the images or his ears to Lindsey's satisfied moans and squeals of pleasure. Her husky, aroused voice stirred the fire in his blood like nothing ever had. Heated pressure pooled low in his belly.

He needed to be involved in this relationship. As much as he resented it, and although he didn't understand how, he was mentally and emotionally linked to her. Nothing had rung normal in his life or Rourke's for the last year, so why not add one more freaky thing to the rest?

Hearing Rourke's deep voice encourage her to climax made Dane harder, so hard his cock ached. But nothing hurt as much as hearing her scream out Rourke's name when she came. His stomach lurched, wishing it was his name. The corrosive envy built in his heart like a jealous acid eating away at his soul.

Some deeper need in him called out to her, too. Something made him aware that Rourke brought her around again, sucking her nipples and encouraging her arousal with his talented hands.

When Dane didn't think he could stand the jealous pain any longer, suddenly, Lindsey filled his mind with tantalizing images of the three of them.

Hell, she was aware of him and his need.

He felt the heat of her mouth on his, her lips nibbling, her tongue tangling with his as her mind probed his, touching memories and uncovering secret desires. Still, he didn't really understand where she was headed, not until he felt her hand replace his on his cock. He sensed her soft, naked skin dragging down along his as she went to her knees and took his cock in her mouth, sucking, stroking, drawing him deep down her throat and close to the edge. He groaned as her lush body brushed against his and his hands tangled in her long, flowing hair.

He cupped his balls and ran his hand up his cock, stroking his hard-on to ease his need, and adjusted himself. He knew she felt him touching himself while he waited outside her room, and he couldn't resist the next stroke or the next. The whole time she resided in his mind and participated, her tongue teased and her hot mouth engulfed him, sucking his cock with a tantalizing stroke and rhythm he'd never experienced before. Near to bursting with desire, Dane pumped his hips harder, faster, and finally exploded, cum filling his hand inside his shorts.

There'd been no stopping it.

God, what a hot mouth. Hell, he'd come like a rank amateur with her inside his head while he'd listened to his brother riding her to completion inside the room.

Yeah, he was disgusted with himself, but her body and mouth had felt so real. Almost as real as the mental link between them. A part of her called out to both of them. Although he couldn't ever remember being attracted to anyone the way he was toward her, his feelings were more than pure sexual attraction. He couldn't deny he felt like he belonged with her. She filled a part of him he hadn't known was missing until he'd met her.

When he realized she could touch his mind, he

didn't bother to wonder *how* it was possible anymore, only *why* if he couldn't have her. She'd searched him out, desiring the mental attachment to him as much as he had.

How could she do this when she obviously belonged to Rourke?

He heard them inside his mind. He felt what they felt. He ached as she whispered kisses over Rourke's chest. He burned while Rourke tasted her. He died a little inside, knowing she was engaged with Rourke, really fucking Rourke, not him.

She wasn't his. Didn't belong to him.

If so, then how did he feel Lindsey's desire reach out for him, too?

How? No. What he really wondered was why. The how was through the strange bond he and Rourke had formed the summer the teens had made their blood-brother pledge. The why was that maybe she felt it, too.

Chapter Eleven

Dane. Lindsey couldn't stop. She almost choked when she realized what had happened, what she'd just done. What they'd done. It'd felt like he'd really been in here with them, the three of them together, and she'd taken his cock in her hand and in her mouth and feasted on him.

He was gone now and hurting. His pain still lingered and made her throat tight. The entire incident confused her. Two males. She'd been linked to both men during her last orgasm, and it had felt incredible. How was this possible, and why?

"I'll be right back. Then we can take a little nap." Rourke left her in bed and went to the bathroom. "Is this woodsy shampoo all you have?"

She squirmed out of the bed and walked to the window, needing a moment alone. "Besides the floral-scented one? Yes."

No nap. Her succubus was gaining power, coming into herself. At this point, until Rourke shifted and grew in strength, she couldn't sleep with him. He'd never withstand mating with her in his dreams. She had to leave Rourke before he started to doze. If his human essence fell asleep with her, she was afraid her uncontrolled nature might consume him.

Now that she'd seen his true human side, she wasn't sure she could control herself, and she wouldn't risk losing that loving side of him. Her control was never much good when she was as distracted as she had been lately. Perhaps now wasn't the best time to test her ability to hold back the succubus since everything at the moment seemed to distract her.

What had happened to all her good intentions and her plans, and why the hell hadn't Rourke used the condoms?

She snatched her bathing suit, putting it on as she ran from the room. Where could she hide from him? Nowhere, since he'd taken her blood.

For now, she'd go into the nearby forest to think, and maybe later, she'd call for Celia. Fat chance she'd get a reasonable explanation. The one fae who knew the future couldn't see how the present fit in, and that could be maddening. No one ever expected a straight answer from Celia. Lindsey didn't know why she expected more. Her aunt would rather have everyone figure out their own fates for themselves.

****

After running for a half hour, Lindsey escaped behind the faery Veil, hoping for a break. If Rourke was what she believed, he'd be able to track her and pass through the invisible Veil that led to the Other world portals. She collapsed on the bank along a nearby brook, hidden away from him for now.

The ground beneath her vibrated, practically hummed with delight as Rourke approached. The Veil wouldn't protect her from him for long, not if he intended to find her. A little time, that's all she'd wanted—or needed—to sort out her feelings about the bond she discovered she had with both Dane and Rourke. Unfortunately, Rourke had a different idea in mind, and his very alpha attitude affected the Veil.

The leaves on the trees whispered, and the forest animals scampered to safety. Apparently even the Earth goddess recognized the man's inner powers. He'd already learned how to use his strength to his advantage and didn't even know he was doing it. Lindsey had to admit he was a quick study.

So why wasn't she surprised?

Nothing about him surprised her anymore. He'd passed through the Veil without a ripple. He was definitely Other.

She wasn't shocked by how easily he found her, only by how quickly. After taking her blood, he could track her anywhere, even if he didn't know it yet.

Despite the frown on his face, the sight of him made the breath catch in her chest. He'd showered. Beads of water sparkled in spots on his forehead, indicating he'd rushed when he found her missing. The little hitch in her heart warmed her when she realized that.

Sniffing the air, she noticed he'd used the woodsy-scented soap. Although he'd tied his hair back, it was still damp and shiny in the light. She hadn't thought he could look any better than he did naked, but she was wrong. He looked equally fantastic in or out of clothes. With his chest bare, he wore only his bathing suit hanging low on his narrow hips, hugging his sturdy thighs like a second skin. She decided she liked the overall effect, right down to his bare feet. She smiled. Bare feet confirmed haste.

Coming after her in bare feet seemed like an act of desperation. The fact that the thought pleased her said so much more than she wanted to acknowledge about her feelings for him. She'd accepted her destiny with him, but she wanted him to desire her, needed that badly, and she planned to kick herself for wanting it later.

He dropped down beside her, and his quiet question sounded like a reprimand. "Why did you leave me?"

Lust ran rampant through her from just the sight of him, especially after having experienced all of his charms firsthand. And yet looking at his bare feet next to hers struck her as staggeringly more intimate than everything else that had gone before. Her insides flamed.

She forced herself to look away from him to hide her raging desire.

"Is it because I bit you and drew blood? I don't know what's gotten into me lately, but I couldn't stop."

"No! No, that was okay. I remembered the safeword."

"But it was your first time." He seemed distracted when he ran his hand across his chest. "Damn it, I shouldn't have gotten so rough."

"No, it's not that at all, really." She touched a hand to her neck where he'd bitten her. The spot ached with the same needy sensation she felt between her thighs. "I needed some alone time."

"You're sure?" His brow knit with concern. "But we weren't finished."

His concern touched her. "That's all. Time." It was hard enough not to admit to herself how much the sight of him affected her. She didn't want to spill her guts to him and give him so much more power over her. "It's nothing like you think."

She decided to be honest. "You know, Rourke, you were right about the first time. About my feelings, I mean. The connection. I just needed some space to sort through my emotions. I was feeling overwhelmed." She didn't like admitting it, but she did think he would understand this one thing.

He gave her a crooked grin. "If that's all it is," he said, pulling her toward him, "you can have space later. You won't feel any different about it forty years from now. Your first is always your first."

That endearing smile of his hit her like a freight train. He kissed her neck and sent flames shooting through to her core. Her pussy clenched. The corners of his eyes crinkled when he smiled at her. She could handle anything but that. The man proved more disarming by the second.

Twisting her into his arms, he slammed her back against his body, trapping her against him. He was already hard, maybe still from before. As far she knew, maybe he was always hard. She hadn't seen him any other way since the first time she'd set eyes on him.

Her body responded quickly when he spread her legs with his knee, pressing his erection insistently against her ass. Rourke nuzzled her hair, inhaling deeply, releasing a slight moan against her neck. She whimpered when his lips touched her ear and his teeth nibbled. Her hips shifted back, responding to the sensation of having his cock so close to where she wanted it.

Move it a little to the right, her succubus screamed. *Stick it in. Fill me. Fuck me. Now!*

The sexual tension building inside her made her want to strip and bend over for him. Her skin tightened, and her canines extended inside her mouth. The shift threatened. The wolf in her instinctively recognized his scent now that he'd marked her. It was her turn to mark him.

This kind of blood bonding was risky if he didn't really care for her, yet despite knowing all she knew, her traitorous hair responded to him, whipping around in the light breeze and ensnaring him to her. And the tattooed wings rippled beneath the skin across her back. She had to get herself under control or give herself away and chance exposing too much too soon.

He held both of her hands with one of his, reached into his pocket, and pulled out a line of foil wrappers. Dangling them in front of her face, he said, "We forgot to use the damn condoms."

His complaint, nothing but grumbled words against her skin, seemed halfhearted. The sound of his deep voice reverberated through her chest, making it more difficult to hold back her wolf.

"I know," she whispered, "but you'll be okay." She shook her head, willing him to leave her, but she returned to the comfort of his arms.

"No, I won't." He was adamant. There was a hint of frustration in his voice, but he looked dazed and sounded astonished when he added, "Something happened to me. I came inside you."

"I'm disease-free and not fertile. There's nothing to worry about."

"Really? How do you know *I* don't have something?"

Oh, you have something, all right. "Do you?" she snapped.

"No. I've never had unprotected sex before." He

shook his head. "I don't know what got into me."

"Good, then there's nothing to—"

He jerked her against him and pressed his body more firmly to hers, his breath a whisper against her cheek. "I'd planned on using the whole box with you before we were done."

His words had her succubus cheering and her heart hoping. Having him so close, feeling his hard, muscled body trembling for control overpowered her defenses. She wanted him as much as he wanted her, maybe more.

"Now we don't need to worry about it. Do we?" she asked.

He simply agreed. "You're right."

The feel of his shaft pressing firmly between her thighs, pressing against her clit, made her want to smile. She couldn't help wanting him again, couldn't help being pleased at his response to her.

Her nails grew longer, digging into the palms of her hands where she'd fisted them. And even though his half-grin melted her insides, she refused to give in. She stood up, and he rose, too, winding his arms around her.

"I have to go." There was no way she was ready to reveal what she was or deal with his innate ability to bring her to her knees.

When she tried to step away, he gripped her tighter and tugged the bikini top's string with his teeth.

"I had plans for today," she explained. Any excuse would do.

"So do I. Mine are better than yours, and I promise, we're not finished by a long shot." His voice was deep, his words a warning. When he cupped her naked breast, his smile conveyed the promise

She sighed. "Really, Rourke—"

"You're hiding something." He slipped his hand inside her bathing suit bottom. "Oh, darlin', I'm so ready to be inside you." He pulled her T-back down her thighs and off. "Turn around. Open up."

She couldn't answer, couldn't breathe as his words set her insides on fire. He wrapped his arms around her from behind, and when his hand touched her mound, she collapsed against him, her back to his chest. She hoped she could tap down her secret while she did as he commanded.

His hand slowly circled her abdomen, lowering her back down to the ground. He groaned in her ear, the sound of his desire mixed with satisfaction. "I want to drive deeper inside you this time. I want to touch your very core."

As his words wove magic, his fingers probed the cleft at the juncture between her thighs, and the blaze consumed her. She let her head fall forward and her eyes roll closed, embracing the guilty pleasure riding over her.

"You're so hot and wet. I want to be inside you right now." His words sounded gruff with passion. "I can't wait to fuck you again."

She wanted him to want her, but she wanted it to really be *him* truly wanting *her*. If this was all just damn fate, it wouldn't be enough. Not for her. Certainly never for him. He was right when he told her she wouldn't walk away from the man who first took her—not without caring. Yet somehow, she knew it wouldn't have mattered. Deep in her heart, she believed it was the fact that the first man had been Rourke. That was what made her care.

He sniffed her neck and slid one finger inside her. She arched her back, leaning into his one hand as his other crept up her body, cupping her breast and fondling her nipple. "What is it, Lindsey? What made me crazy for you after the first time? You're creamy fire in my hands, and I know you want this as much as I do."

He wanted *her*. She hoped it wasn't the binding making him feel that way. She touched her lips to his. She needed the truth. A sharp nip to the corner of his lips made him wild with desire. As she sucked droplets of his rich blood, his cock nudged harder into her soft flesh, and he licked his own blood from her mouth.

She sensed the aching sexual need rise up in him, and her succubus responded, begging for release. *Let me pleasure him this time. You had him last time.*

Lindsey rolled on top of Rourke, allowing her fae succubus free for the first time. She hoped she could handle a virgin succubus, and if she couldn't, she had to believe Rourke could.

"Let yourself go, Rourke. Enjoy the moment. You know how much joy you give me with your body. Allow me to return the favor, at least this one time."

"How many men are going to turn down an offer like that?"

"You might. I know how you like to be the one in control."

With a shimmer, her glamour surrounded them. The luminous light dazzled him, and faery dust swirled like a tornado.

"Well, baby. I'm all yours this time. Give it your best shot, because I'm taking control after this and not ever giving it back."

"We'll see about that."

He'd taken her blood without really realizing what he had done, and now she would have to take more of his. She hated doing it this way, but she had to enthrall him before binding him to her with his blood.

"Pzshwiest!" A whispered magical word in his ear, one he'd never be able to pronounce, would have him thinking this was a dream. The wings on her back popped free as she lowered herself onto his cock. They wrapped around Rourke much as her arms and her hair did, caressing him.

"God, you feel wonderful. I take it back. You can take control like this anytime." His hands explored her crevices while she tried to please him with every trick her succubus knew.

"I really love your hair. It feels like the tendrils are embracing me, touching me like butterfly wings, stroking my skin."

"Oh, Rourke, are you waxing poetic on me? I'll never be able to resist that. The fae love a poet's soul."

He grunted a response she didn't hear when he touched her clit and rubbed. She reared back and gasped as he mumbled, "Fae? I thought you were a succubus."

All conscious thought flew away. So much for control.

She licked her lip again and tried to probe his mind. She was a succubus for crying out loud, and the man was seducing her again. She needed an idea of what he liked. Her fae magic should be able to work when his guard was down.

She slipped through his mental blocks, and Lindsey scrolled through sexual images from his mind until she found the ones that turned him on most. Her body burned with desire as she imagined being with him in all those ways. "Your hands are so hot, I need you to—" She moaned.

What? What did she need?

"Tell me, what do you need, baby? I want to give it to you."

"This." She impaled herself on his rock-hard erection and sighed as she slid down his length to the base. He groaned. Her eyes closed and rolled open with pleasure when she was fully seated.

Rourke grinned up at her, oblivious to her wings, too mesmerized by the myriad of colors and variety of sensations she created for his pleasure. Once in his head, she had pulled out more of his favorite fantasies, and now she fed them back to him.

Lost in the moment of ecstasy, Rourke only managed a low mumble as he threw his head back, arching up, driving his cock deeper inside her. She felt him nudge her womb.

"Oh, baby, do you have fingers in there? I feel like a thousand tiny fingers are caressing my cock while you squeeze, hot, slippery, and tight around me."

The feeling of attachment to him shocked her. Every part of her nature wanted to keep him. She hoped taking his blood wasn't a betrayal, but the sight of his masculine, corded throat sent a rush of desire to her core. His hot, thick blood coursing through his veins beneath the pulse beating in his throat sparked a sensation, a dark desire Lindsey hadn't experienced before. The *bloodlust.*

He moaned as she rode him. Her hunger called to her, refusing to be denied. Her sharp, pointed canines caught against her tongue as she tried to ignore the bloodlust. The temptation was too great to resist.

She lowered her mouth to his throat and bit him, drawing on him as he came, and then as the taste of his blood filled her mouth her orgasm exploded. This time, she cried out his name as he yelled out hers, and the sound of their satisfied pleasure echoed through the fae forest.

Then she whispered, "You are for me, Rourke Grayland."

Chapter Twelve

Lindsey dropped the glamour, and the light dimmed as she collapsed on top of Rourke's chest. *What have we done?*

"It's time to spit it out." Rourke lifted her chin and watched her response with narrowed eyes. "What are you hiding from me?"

Before he'd taken her blood, she could have prevented him from finding her and touching her mind. She couldn't hide anything from him now. But after taking his blood, she figured they were even again. She smiled. "I could ask the same of you." And she kissed him on the nose.

"You walked away from me. I can't walk away from you," he said. "It goes against my grain to feel this way."

Her hackles rose at his arrogance. "Grain or pride?" She stood up and walked to the stream.

"Grain, pride, it's all the same, isn't it?" He approached her and drew her into his arms.

"Ah, well, there, that's one of my problems. You think all my responses are about you. Maybe that's what's wrong. Your pride." She dropped her head to his chest and listened to the strong, steady beat of his heart.

"No. It's not that. You were already aware of that side of me the minute you saw me. It's more." He sniffed her. "You smell like... I don't know. Heaven.

Or hell. Sex and sin."

"Sin?"

"I can't decide. The sex feels too much like sin to be heaven and too good to be hell." His embrace on her tightened. "But wanting you like this… This feels like hell. Everything about you is pure sex. Your body is made for sin. I can't resist you."

She turned away. "Maybe that's my problem, too. I'm feeling the same way about you, torn between fighting this strong attraction and succumbing to it."

He turned her around to face him and studied her. "You do want me as much as I want you." He pulled her tight inside his embrace. "I thought it was just me. I'm confused, in a constant state of arousal around you, and shit, I'm hard all the time."

She glanced down. "I was wondering about that."

"I can smell the honey pouring out of your folds again, even now. It's almost like I can hear your arousal screaming for me to satisfy you. Why can't we get enough of each other?"

She wasn't prepared for his questions or the way his powerful mind probed hers. Despite the barriers she'd erected to keep him out, his mind drove through her defenses and merged with hers, looking for answers, stealing into her memories as well as her thoughts. In the middle of his declaration and in the middle of their passionate embrace, she'd never expected his mind to invade hers, picking out the one memory that could hurt him beyond measure—his past.

No. But he was there inside her mind, taking the information from her. As much as she tried, she couldn't keep him from delving deeper, touching the knowledge that could destroy his relationship with

Dane.

Seeing the confusion hit Rourke's face as he merged with her mind made her wonder how strong he really was.

"What's going on? Why do I feel linked to you? It's stronger than my feelings for Dane. I'd always figured he and I were close because we've been together since birth."

She took a few steps away, not wanting him to see the fear in her eyes. If he had a mental connection to Dane, maybe that's why she was drawn to both men.

He turned her to face him and held her by her upper arms. His brow furrowed. His eyes shifted, looking around first then piercing hers, accepting their mental link, and more too easily.

Maybe he saw the confusion on her face or heard her concern in his mind, but he answered her unspoken question. "Strange things have been happening to me lately. I came here looking for answers, and I plan to get them. So if you know something, tell me."

"Are you sure you're ready?" The answers she had for him could obliterate the last shred of his humanity.

"I can't live with nothing but questions."

"I guess you're right." Lindsey worried about the consequences of upsetting him. If he shifted completely before they finished the Beltane ceremony, she didn't know what would happen to them. But more than anxiety over the legends drove her concern. After making love to him, she didn't relish the thought of bringing him the kind of pain the shared visions of the past would cause. They would wound Rourke in a way no mortal injury could, and above all, she didn't want to be the one to deliver the blow.

The masculine control entered her mind, and he innocently pulled at her memories, not comprehending what he was doing. She fought him, trying to block him from her thoughts, but after the blood exchange, she was naked to him, body and mind.

No matter how hard she tried, Lindsey couldn't stop envisioning the tale of his past as it had been told to her by Zeelane, the old fae Seer.

"Show me." Rourke demanded when her reluctance forced his hand. He was a quick study.

A vision of a wolf standing in a clearing appeared in her mind, no matter how hard she tried to hold it back.

The wolf nuzzled a baby wrapped in a blanket. The action quieted him before she took off to chase the hare she'd scented hiding in the nearby brush.

Lindsey envisioned the strange birthmark on the babe's back. It was smaller, but the same as Rourke's, a winged dragon.

Next came a vision of a hunter.

The sound of the crying baby must have drawn the hunter to them, and thinking to protect the human child from danger, the man raised his rifle, took aim, and then came the resounding flash of a gunshot.

Rourke's eyes burst open when the wolf dropped to the ground, and he shuddered as if the bullet had hit him.

Lindsey closed her eyes, shivered, and ran her hands up her arms. The scent of blood, metallic and warm, sent a knife of ice to her heart.

Nothing could warm her or him. Her thoughts and her emotions flowed from her into Rourke, and she watched his expression change as those visions held him trapped in the horror.

She sent her aura to enfold him, but nothing soothed him.

The shock of that moment filled her as if she'd been there. More images of that evening in the forest flashed inside her head, and Rourke held her thoughts captive despite the pain the images caused him. He wouldn't let her stop the kaleidoscope of events flashing through their minds, not now. Not when the truth was about to become clear—ice cold and crystalline.

The wolf collapsed, and as she did, the hunter staggered as she shifted back into her human form in a growing pool of blood.

The woman lay dying, and she was all the evidence the hunter needed to finally believe that the old mountain tales were indeed true. Shifters existed.

Lindsey mentally noted, almost to appease Rourke, that the hunter tried to help the dying woman. His thoughts were confused, frustrated, frightened.

Dying? The shot was off. The wound hadn't been a killing shot.

No, it shouldn't have been deadly, yet the woman was mortally wounded, and her life force was fading fast.

Rourke dropped his forehead to Lindsey's as the events continued in slow motion, and the ache inside her heart grew along with his pain. *"Why is she dying?"*

Images of the man preparing the bullets formed in their minds.

He sat at a table and used silver in his casing mixture for these bullets, because silver was more plentiful in the mountain near his home than any other metal.

Silver. Deadly to the shifter.

The hunter tried to aid the wounded woman. She exhaled, reached out one last time to the crying babe, collapsed, and with her last breath uttered, "Hide him from the dragon."

The man looked at the woman's body and then back at the baby, a horrified expression on his face. Fear filled his eyes, and Lindsey could only imagine his regrets.

Appalled, devastated. Whose feelings were these?

Lindsey realized the hunter had been shocked when the truth about the mountains' myths slammed home. Secondly, he'd been saddened. He'd killed a young mother, leaving her child helpless.

Tears spilled down the man's face as he dug the shallow grave. Then he buried the woman and crept back to his home, bringing the baby to his recently delivered wife. Without question or explanation, she took the newborn in her arms and nursed him beside her own infant.

There was no doubt the other baby was Dane when he turned to examine Rourke, exposing his dimpled smile.

Lindsey didn't have to read Rourke's mind to understand how he felt. His emotions were linked to hers. Confusion and anger escalated inside him. Furious. Rourke held her head in place, and he shuddered with the knowledge. Heartache, pain, and resolution clearly tore at his emotions.

The one thing she didn't find was denial. Why was that?

"Tell me what's really going on," he demanded.

"How'd you get inside my head?" Lindsey countered.

He ignored her question. "What are you?"

"Fae, wolf-shifter, succubus," Lindsey whispered. "Maybe the question we should be asking is what are *you*?"

"Explain."

"You know what I am, and I am for you."

"Then it is your responsibility to tell me the truth."

He insisted she be the one to hurt him. Hadn't the pain she had already caused him been enough? "First, tell me what it is about you that has you taking all this in stride. Most humans couldn't accept the Lore this easily."

"Things have never been normal for me. So tell me what you know and fill in the blank spaces in my life."

"Shortly after the incident, the Graylands ran, losing themselves in the crowded city. Your very existence was masked from us—you among so many humans. He hid you in the concrete high-rise mountains. He did as your mother wished."

"Why?"

"I don't know. Maybe it had something to do with her husband, Rafe, or with your biological father. If anyone knows the truth, no one is telling me."

Lindsey's final visions were of Grayland taking his family and fleeing the forest. All these years later, she couldn't find it in her heart to blame him for what fate had done to him. Grayland's fear of the repercussions of stealing Rourke, not to mention his newly acquired knowledge of the forest's secret, must have been alarming, especially with the responsibility of the female shifter's death resting so heavily on his shoulders.

"Who would know?"

"Maybe the Council or my aunt Celia, but then, I don't know if anyone knows about the details of your past. Maybe the forest fae, but I've never heard them speculate." She shook her head. "Sorry."

"I should go ask them."

"No, Rourke, you shouldn't. You won't be welcomed into the Otherworld until after Beltane, until after you commit to this world. Despite how everything started, you and Dane are soul brothers. You became friends and business partners. You've influenced the world of enterprise without the knowledge of your past, without an inkling that magic exists or of the fate that awaits you."

"Nothing awaits me."

Lindsey shook her head and turned away from him with a shrug. "Destiny is destiny. Believe what you want."

"I know what Dane and I are and aren't to each other. What we've accomplished. And fate?" He spun her around and shook her gently by her shoulders. "Well, fate can go fuck itself. I do what I want. I'm not going to be guided by some Council's idea of my destiny. I owe nothing to my world or your Otherworld from what I can tell so far."

A heart could crack open and bleed. The statement she'd been waiting for hurt more than she'd expected.

Rourke dropped his hands and stood, stone-faced, giving away nothing, blocking her from his feelings.

She nodded. Yes, that's the way she'd expected him to react. "Not all this came as a surprise to you.

Why? You're taking too much of this in stride." Something about his response made her wonder. "Did you already know you weren't biological brothers?"

The two men owned and headed up a genetic research company. Of course they knew. Rourke was CEO, and Dane managed the research department. Genetic research. She figured they'd expect proof, not speculations. Unless they already had it.

"Yeah, we knew. Old paternity test." Rourke cocked his head to one side and almost managed to look sheepish. "Like I said, until you, I always used condoms. So does Dane. We did the same girl, together, and she came up pregnant. After extensive testing, the sperm that produced her baby didn't hail from either of us. Hell, we already knew that, and thankfully, the tests proved it, but they also revealed one other bit of interesting info." He looked straight into her eyes. "Something was weird with our DNA, and we weren't even brothers, let alone twins."

She gasped. "*Both* of your DNA is *weird*?"

"Yup. No one ever saw anything like it. We didn't tell anyone where the samples came from, of course. It's Dane's pet project now. His was different than mine, but neither of ours tested entirely human."

Both of them? Maybe that's why she responded to Dane, too. Had destiny preordained both males for Lindsey? "I didn't know about Dane. I don't think anyone does. This could affect everything."

Rourke's laugh had an edge. "It doesn't affect me."

Dane's human father had done the unforgivable—killed Rourke's mother, stealing his life and his heritage from him. "I wonder... Did Dane's father claim a young shifter wife without knowing it? How did she conceal her gift from her husband?"

"Maybe she went visiting relatives once a month," Rourke said with a note of sarcasm.

"Whether you believe me or not, this isn't something you can deny. Running away won't change anything, Rourke."

"What makes you so sure I'll shift?"

"Your mother, to start. Your dragon birthmark, the other. Your mother's husband, Rafe, found the evidence of her murder—her body buried in the shallow grave. While he was searching for his family that evening, the forest fae revealed the gruesome details to him, and he told the Council. Then everyone kept your disappearance and your mother's death a secret. No one told me why your mother wanted you hidden.

"For years, Rafe searched for you among the human towns nearby, but Grayland had hidden you and his family well within the mortal world. Rafe never did learn your whereabouts before his death this year. Sarah's death and your abduction were concealed from everyone for all these years, but after his death, the world of the Others bordered on chaos, and the forest fae revealed the other secret to the Council. You were alive.

"Next Beltane, when Aryan, the dragon-shifter, discovers Sarah and Rafe's deaths, he'll return. We will all only have the hope of the prophecy that says our leader will return. Aryan will go through the bloodlust again if he's not stopped. He gets stronger with each kill."

"Aryan is a dragon-shifter? Like a big, huge dragon?"

"Yes, according to legend, a killing machine. A

dragon without conscience." She nodded.

"How do you figure I fit in?"

"I don't know how you fit in. Your whereabouts have only recently been discovered." She touched his back over the spot where his birthmark was. "This must mean something."

"What do you think I have to do with a dragon-shifter? Not that I'm going to be involved. I'm just curious. I'm really not the joiner type."

"I've only recently been told of my part in all this." She stopped mid-thought. "Let me see your back."

"No problem, babe. I'll show you mine if you show me yours, but the interesting stuff's not on my back. Come a little closer—"

"Stop fooling around. Let me make something clear, Rourke. All the forest people believe the time of the Legend is upon us. Our wolf prince will return. Some think that's you. After what you just told me, I think it's Dane. Whether you believe in this or not, the foretold return is imminent. All the signs point to a change. I was summoned here to fulfill my part and, I believe, so were you."

She tapped his birthmark. "This is the sign of the dragon."

"How so?"

"Rourke, before Beltane you'll begin to shift. You may have already noticed your body practicing. But on that night you will turn thirty and will come into your full powers. Shift—"

"Into a wolf?" He laughed.

"Yes, but you may start before then." She nodded. "More than that, I think Aryan may have sired you. If he was your biological father, you may shift into the dragon. Now, with Dane in the mix, I'm not sure what all this means."

"You think Dane will shift, too? He hasn't had any of the same symptoms."

"What symptoms?"

"I've been experiencing some signs of aggression. You already know about my sexual tastes. Biting, blood, and rough sex."

She smirked.

"Don't laugh. I'm getting worse daily."

"Anything else?"

"My appetite. I want my red meat bloody, and I pass on almost everything else lately."

"Your eyes. Have they changed?"

"My eyes, my face, and my skin look different, and my throat burns and aches like hell from time to time."

"I've never heard of those symptoms all occurring in one male. You must be miserable."

"I'm cranky and frustrated, wishing I could run naked and wild. And there's something else…"

"What?"

"I…I dream of flying—" He glanced to the sky. "—soaring over mountains and valleys."

"Flying?" Lindsey practically jumped off the ground. "Wolf-shifters don't imagine flying. Eagle-shifters and avian-shifters do, but I've never heard of a wolf-shifter envisioning flying. A dragon might."

"If that's what I am, then they do."

"We don't know what you're capable of for sure and won't know until we find out who sired you. We know you're wolf because your mother was, and you are alpha because her father was the local pack leader until her mate took his place. She was already carrying you when Rafe claimed her, but he never revealed that he wasn't your biological father until his death. You say you're also something else according to your DNA tests. Could your father have been part human male?"

He shrugged. "Maybe. The tests showed human DNA, lupine, and something else that resembled reptile and avian DNA. I'm a mutt."

"Reptile and avian? A dragon."

"Aryan?" he asked.

She nodded.

"We exchanged blood, Rourke. Do you know what that means?"

"Whatever I am, so are you?" He grinned a big, toothy smile. "Does that work the other way, too? So am I a succubus?"

"Incubus. Males are called incubi," she snapped back. "You're really not taking this all seriously enough."

His face went dark. "Oh, I'm taking all of this very seriously. Don't get me wrong."

"The Council of Others hopes you'll take your rightful place in the Council and in the pack as leader, replacing your father."

"He wasn't my father. Did your Council think about that?"

"No, but your biological great-grandfather was the pack Congress leader in any case. He was the alpha wolf over every pack in the Southwest. You were conceived to lead."

He laughed again. "Your Council couldn't be more wrong about me. You know, you're all in deep shit if you think I'm here to save your world."

"It's your world, too."

Great! He seemed to be taking all this Lore stuff in stride, but wait until he found out he'd already instinctively united them to each other. All hell would break loose. That was a piece of information she intended to keep from him as long as she could. Hopefully, fate wouldn't tear them all apart.

"We need to find Dane and fill him in. Tell him about what he could be, the situation, how he might be involved," she said.

"What's the extent of your interest?"

"He could be in trouble. Other than that, I don't know why I'm worried about him. What exactly are you asking?

"I'm asking you if you're attracted to Dane."

"Yes, I'm attracted to Dane. I can't deny that I feel more than just platonic concern for him. Honestly, I don't understand my feelings. The connection I have to you both confuses me. I somehow feel his needs, his desire, and his emotions when I'm with you. It's as if he completes us."

Highly agitated by her answer, Rourke walked away and turned his back. "I won't share you. The thing inside me won't stand for it."

"Okay, I understand, but it may be a matter of life or death for Dane. It also may be a matter of life or death for us."

He rubbed his eyes. "I can't think straight. My vision is off. Something's happening."

Lindsey searched the sky. The moon began to rise low on the eastern horizon. Early. The sun wasn't even close to setting yet. "You might already be experiencing the effects of the moon. We don't have much time before you shift. Anything could set it off now. Fear, anger, any deep emotion."

"Jealousy?"

"Yes. Are you feeling—?"

"The beast inside me is. Dane and I are used to sharing women, but apparently, this guy inside me has other ideas. He's very possessive. Every time the subject comes up, I want to kill someone and fuck you brainless until you can't think about another man touching you."

"Rourke, it's not like that. You satisfy me completely, but Dane feels like a part of us."

"No, you can't be with him. I can't risk hurting him. You have to promise me you'll stay away from other men for now, especially Dane." He grew thoughtful. "Especially him, at least until I get this…this beast inside me under control."

"I can't promise what I'll do. I'm new at this, too. It's not in my nature."

"Which nature?"

"You know what I am. I'm a shifter, a wolf, but I am also a fae and a succubus. Nothing about any of my natures rings monogamous. Unless my bond mate claims me for all times, I will be as promiscuous as my nature deems. I won't be able to stop myself. I will have to fuck or die."

"You were a virgin?"

"This is the time of *my* rising, too. Like you, I'm experiencing some of my changes for the first time. Unlike you, I've been raised in the Lore and trained for all this. I've been undergoing transition for years in preparation for…you." She tapped back her thoughts. *My bond mate.*

"Me, specifically?"

"No." Lindsey smiled. "Someone. *The* one."

Rourke growled, the jealousy rising in him again. "Me. No one else. Not Dane. Promise!"

"I told you, I can't. I'm not sure what we're meant to be to each other or what we're meant to do. But I'll find out and protect him. I won't let anything happen to him." She reached up and cupped his hard jaw in her hands. "Rourke, I won't let you hurt him. I can promise you that."

His gaze rolled down her body. "Thanks for the thought, but under the circumstances, you won't blame me for still worrying. You wouldn't be much of a challenge if I wanted to overpower you, so you'd hardly be a match for what's inside me. Especially if it's the dragon."

"Don't worry, I can handle myself. I may look slight, but my powers are growing as Beltane approaches."

"What powers, little girl?"

"What? You need a demonstration? That's ridiculous. I don't want to flex my muscles for you."

"Humor me. Show me the power, so I feel relieved."

Lindsey didn't have all the control over her powers she'd hoped for yet. This demonstration was foolish. But she needed Rourke to understand she'd keep Dane safe. "Okay."

She let the power fill her. The glamour intensified, and her mind control wrapped around Rourke's thoughts, bringing him to his knees. She trapped his mind and took over, instilling visions of wolves and vampires shifting, of dragons flying overhead, of feline shifters and Weres. As they threatened to attack him, she mentally stepped in front of him, guarding him, blocking the danger from him. Even in the illusion, she felt his anger rage at her. How dare she put herself in harm's way for him! How dare his *bond mate* risk her life for him!

The illusion dissipated into mist around them. Lindsey saw the realization in Rourke's eyes. She didn't need to access his thoughts to sense the rage he felt at her betrayal.

"You bound us?" He ground out the question.

"No."

"What do you mean *no?* We are bound, aren't we?"

"Yes. *You* bound us that first time without realizing it."

"Me? I did this? Why didn't you stop me? Why didn't you say something?"

"Ah, I was a little preoccupied at the time. Remember? Virgin, here. I hardly expected *that* of all things from you. What could I say when the deed was already done? Believe me, I was as shocked and confused then as you are now. You think I want to be bound to someone who doesn't want me?"

"Oh, no problem there. That is the problem. I do want you. More than I should. More than I think I would if I hadn't been influenced by…what? What exactly did you do to me?"

"Right, Mr. Tactful. I did something to you? That's just the kind of sweet talking a woman wants to hear. 'You hexed me. I don't want to want you.' Well, I don't want to be the one fate dumped on you, either. How do you like that?"

"I don't like it at all. So we're even."

"Right! Each stuck with someone we don't know if we really want, forever, like it or not."

He staggered in place as if he'd been hit by a two-by-four.

Lindsey knew the outcome of this argument was inevitable. She moved toward him. With the pale moon rising behind him and fury radiating off him, the adrenaline pumping through him would start his change.

"I'm sick." He held out his hand and pushed her away.

Rourke furred up, his expression darkening and his body growing larger.

"It's the change. Here, let me help." She took his shoulders to comfort him.

"No." Rourke growled, and this time, it sounded like the true growl of an alpha male wolf. He batted her hand away and turned from her before he dropped to his knees. "You've helped more than enough. Stay away from me and Dane."

He fell, his body flattened in the grass. Bones crunched and muscles exploded as he lifted himself off the ground to all fours. His glossy, black pelt covered his broad chest and sturdy frame. White facial markings surrounded his muzzle, and his bright golden eyes lent an air of familiarity to the wolf's face as he glared back over his shoulder at her.

"You are magnificent."

His expression screamed with accusation although she wasn't sure what part he blamed on her and which he blamed on fate or himself. In any case, he had, for the moment, rejected her, their bond, and his heritage.

He'd have to return to her eventually, but he

wouldn't take his place in the pack or on the Council until he accepted her.

"Rourke, don't go off. We both sensed another presence inside you. It's not safe for you to be away from me this close to the full moon when your emotions are mixed, not if there is another beast inside you, especially if it's the dragon. The calling brought you here to me for a reason. I am the only one who can help you through your transition."

"Help? You betrayed me." His thoughts said one thing, but maybe she picked up on his emotions, because his expression looked wounded.

"I would never betray you, Rourke."

He snapped at the air and growled at her. Then he ran off, alone, slipping through the Veil into the mortal world just as dusk was falling. A few minutes later, she heard the howl, long and lonely, before she walked through the Veil and turned back to the lodge.

"Run, Rourke, but know this—I am always with you."

Chapter Thirteen

Lindsey knocked on Dane's door, and when he opened it, he acted surprised, as if he were expecting someone else.

He leaned outside and glanced around before turning to her. "I half expected Rourke to push his way inside."

"You were expecting Rourke?" she asked without meeting Dane's eyes.

"Actually, I-I sort of sensed you right before I opened the door. I guess I didn't expect you to be alone...or the impact that seeing you would have on me."

He didn't physically touch her, but she felt his desire just the same, and something else. And in that moment, she knew nothing would prevent him from eventually having her. Not Rourke. Not heaven or hell.

"Where's Rourke?" His eyes narrowed on her.

"He went off by himself to sulk. He's upset, angry."

"About what?" Dane snapped.

"Actually, several things. And he has every right to feel as he does. I told him the story of his beginnings and how you two came to be...brothers."

Lindsey went on explaining to Dane their origins. As she told him about the story of their beginnings, she watched the pain reach deep inside and twist Dane's heart. His expression contorted with emotions. The connection she had with him allowed her to experience his pain and confusion.

When she finished revealing the story of their past, she stood and faced him, toe to toe and stared him straight in the eye. "I suspect you, like Rourke, hate the idea of fate being forced on you. I'm not sure which he's the most upset about—what happened in the past and that he and I are bound to each other against his free will, or this quirky little issue between you and me."

"You told him about—" He studied her and shrugged.

"I told him everything. Though he already knew."

"You are reckless with others' feelings."

"I am not. I didn't do it. The image of us was in my mind when he pulled the memories from me. He's more powerful than I expected."

"Never underestimate Rourke." Dane shook his head and kept shaking it. "I can't be involved—"

"Too late. He knows how much I want you and need you, too." She recognized Dane's denial. She felt the same way about Rourke knowing.

Dane surprised her when he kissed her quiet, and though she fought her emotions for him, her heart raced with reluctant desire. Through their emotional connection, she experienced the heat—his heat, the passion—their passion, the need—their joint need. She couldn't deny it, and now neither could he as she entered his mind and shared her thoughts.

Mine, Dane. You are for me.

His kiss had inflamed her, but when he pushed her away and held her at arm's length, he frowned. "I can't do this to him."

"You don't have a choice. I couldn't promise Rourke that I'd stay away from you. We're destined," she whispered.

"You're killing me," he moaned, pulling her back into the circle of his arms, and then he crushed her against his chest. With his face buried in her hair, he inhaled and murmured, "We're doomed."

"Perhaps. But only if he can't learn to share me." She cupped Dane's face in her hands and held his stare. "You are for me and I am for you. Rourke is ours, too, as we are his. Never doubt our connection or our fate."

****

Oh, Dane wanted Lindsey, all right. Enough to give her up? Maybe. But not likely. Did he care enough to share her? The pain of standing aside was almost unbearable to think about. The connection he felt with her was as strong as his connection with Rourke. He didn't understand how he and Rourke could share emotions unless she was the conduit.

He was suddenly beginning to comprehend the test results and their former relationship. Had they been dipping into this connection all along?

Dane's ears perked up at the sound of pack wolves howling in the distance.

Lindsey turned in the direction of the howls. "We have to find him. He could be in danger."

That was all Dane needed to know. "Think about him. Help me track him. I'll go."

"I don't think he fully understands what he's up against. He needs me with him—oh. Stop me. I'm rambling."

"You help me, and I'll take it from here. He may

come back looking for you. Stay right here until I return. I know how to talk to him. I'll find him and bring him back to you. We have always had a sixth sense between each other, and now, with your help, it can be stronger."

The sun was already sinking lower on the horizon when Dane left Lindsey to hunt Rourke. The sounds of howling wolves filling the air with their threats irritated him. Rourke claimed wolves weren't native to this area, not likely to venture this far south, but the constant howling proved otherwise, didn't it? When he eventually found him, Dane would take great pleasure rubbing his brother's face in his mistake. So rare an opportunity shouldn't be overlooked.

The farther he ventured into the hills, the sounds of the pack grew closer. All the while, he concentrated his thoughts and directed them at Rourke while Lindsey sent him strengthening support.

He did a quick double take, glancing around for cover. No place to run, no low branches to climb. He checked behind him, over his shoulder. What was he expecting? Backup? Not likely out here. When he spotted the pack, they turned out to be only two gray wolves with murder in their eyes, and he was the only prey in the area. Jeez, he'd never realized wolves got that large.

He was in big trouble when a third one came out of the trees and changed in front of his eyes. The creature stood up on his haunches, taller than any normal man. This was no ordinary wolf. Dane let out the breath he'd been holding.

No, this was a huge beast, bigger than any he'd ever imagined. The damn thing snarled at him out of an extraordinarily human looking form. The eyes glaring at him were those of a maddened wolf, flame-red, blazing, crazed.

No human in there despite his appearance. That was for certain. The teeth? Pure wolf. The claws on his large human hands matched those of a grizzly bear.

The others shifted.

"Lindsey, if you're out there listening, take shelter or run!"

The attack was so fast Dane didn't see it coming when it started. Once the big one tore at him, the other two joined in, snarling and ripping into his flesh. Dane lost all sense of being until the vision of a white unicorn shimmered within a bright light in front of him. The monsters that had attacked him were nowhere in sight when he tried to lift himself off the forest floor.

He struggled to his feet, trying to orient himself to the forest. He thought of the beasts, not normal wolves, and he thought about Rourke. He hoped the three hadn't gotten to him. Dane had to get back to Lindsey before she came out hunting for him and met up with the beasts.

****

All the revelations Lindsey had shared with him left Rourke almost relieved. Suddenly, he had a few answers to the questions he'd had before he came here.

The mental anguish weighing on him disappeared right after his shift. No guilt, no worries. No pain. Not until her voice whispered in his mind. He'd sensed the trouble as soon as she had. *Dane's in trouble. He went out searching for you and didn't come back.*

Rourke ran. Full out. Through the forest, up the mountain to the summit. This wolf form was pure power and freedom.

It was well after dusk when Rourke heard a rustling in the bushes, and a familiar scent made his nose twitch. Rabbit. Not enough competition for his restless nature tonight. His golden wolf eyes sought out a more challenging prey in the dim light of the forest. Yes, they were there, watching, ready to strike. Ready to test him.

Wolves. Rogues.

Rourke sensed the other shift threatening, the one worrying him in his human form, the one that didn't concern him now.

The darkness in him was anxious to turn, but even he knew it was too soon. The pale moon wasn't quite full as it approached its zenith in the evening sky, but later this week, when it was, he wouldn't be able to prevent the inevitable change. Keeping the scary beast at bay grew more difficult as his emotions escalated and the full moon approached.

When he'd shifted into the wolf, he'd barely been able to stop there. Something wanted out, something frightening and powerful had tried to escape. Now, it threatened again.

His giant, furry, black head snapped to attention when he caught the scent of the other predators' approach. He smelled the pack.

Come on, guys, make my day! The gray wolf pack started circling the tree line where he stood inside the open patch, waiting. He needed this fight, an outlet to hold back whatever beast dwelled within him. He needed this savage hunt to quell the desperate violence mounting inside him.

If they thought he was just another lone wolf, they were very mistaken.

Run from me, my cousins, he mentally warned into the night.

He'd tear out their throats and rip them to pieces just because he could. No remorse, no conscience.

No? Then come and get me. You've made your choice to die. There was a joy in taunting them.

The scouts moved in, their growls escalating. One youngster came out of the trees prematurely, giving Rourke the advantage. The larger male wolf growled a steady snarl of reprimand from the perimeter, but it was too late. Then he joined in, simultaneously attacking from the other side.

Rourke circled, first grabbing one by the back of the neck and shaking him, breaking his neck and tossing his body aside while he slashed out with his claws at the other. His greater size and strength slammed the young wolf's body into the large pine beside him.

He welcomed the attack.

Meet your dark death, traitor. Your blood will rid me of the bloodlust for the moment, and as I kill each one of you, I will take your spirit and send it to the Underworld where those who betray their own belong.

The second wolf jumped Rourke from behind. He flipped the large male over his body and sliced his throat as he tossed him through the air.

With the blood of the kills dripping from his claws and muzzle, Rourke felt himself shifting again. This time, the transformation felt different. His body grew longer, taller, not man, not wolf. Was he turning into some other kind of monster?

Where the hell was this transformation going?

His chest exploded, thick and wide. His snout

broadened, and his wolf pelt shimmered into iridescent, black-pearled scales. Something about them looked familiar. Then he remembered Chicago and the night of the last full moon, his eyes, his teeth, and Amelia screaming beneath him, her blood dripping from his lips.

The cracking and tearing finally stopped, and the lingering ache from his bones separating and shifting dulled to merely an annoyance.

The trees looked shorter.

Rourke estimated his new, muscled body stood over ten feet tall and twenty feet long. His feet were clawed with long, deadly talons. He had wings, and his wingspan had to be over forty feet. The beast roared. A short spark of fire shot past rows of long, jagged teeth, and anger burst to the surface.

Flames blazed from his muzzle. A dragon.

Well, what-da-ya-know! I am *a fucking fire-breathing dragon.* He stretched, shrugged his massive shoulders, spread his enormous talon-tipped wings, and roared again. This time, with purpose. *Wings and all.*

The other wolves must have heard the screams from the earlier attack. The rest of the pack stayed back in the trees but slowly closed in, tightening the circle around Rourke. The alpha came out of the tree line more carefully, and the leader stopped dead in his tracks when he saw Rourke. The remaining wolves dropped to their haunches in submission.

His brother's scent wasn't on any of these wolves. There was another killer out there somewhere.

He turned his back on the wolves. He sensed they were of little consequence as they slinked back into the dark forest, wisely disappearing into the shadows.

Rourke remained in the clearing, trying to gather control, trying to shift out of the dragon and back into one form or other, man or wolf, at least one he knew he could contain.

Chapter Fourteen

A breeze blew past Rourke, and he felt the itch to test his limits. As the moon crept higher, he wondered if he'd have time to try out his wings and fly before the bloodlust returned. Once it returned, he was afraid he'd be lost to rational thinking, his human side completely obliterated by his transformation. Each moment he experienced approaching the full moon brought him closer to the beast and further from his humanity.

Rourke flapped his wings and soared over the forest. A spark of joy flickered within his human soul, and the high pitch of the beast's scream screeched, resounding sharply inside his head and ringing out over the evening skies. The power of the dragon consumed him.

The scent of blood filled his nostrils. The scent smelled familiar. Dane's. Wolf. Man. Three or four creatures. They smelled like a combination of wolf and man, only different. Stronger, wilder, more feral. His brother's blood was on them.

With his dragon vision, he couldn't miss the huge, hulking shadows inside the tree line. Weres. Something told him instinctively what they were, an old knowledge embedded in his DNA, maybe.

The Werewolves headed toward the caves at the base of the mountain. Rourke swooped low over the trees. Their colossal size didn't surprise him. They seemed like giant wolf men with long, flowing hair, wolves walking upright with wolfen eyes and teeth in strangely human features until they turned their empty, rogue eyes at him. They appeared as much like men as wolves; the blend was an exotic contrast. That did surprise him. He imagined the hybrids were Weres, and who could believe they would be so horrifyingly beautiful in their awfulness.

The biggest one reeked of Dane's blood. Agony ripped through the human inside him, dangerously affecting the dragon. If he wanted to attack, this was his last chance before they disappeared into one of the dark holes in the mountain. As the dragon, Rourke was too large to fit, and his rage exploded with his frustration. He was determined to get his revenge.

The beast bellowed. Flames lit the night sky. The man inside cried out, the wolf growled, the dragon screeched. Alone within the dragon, Rourke lost all sense of being as he flew out over the night sky seeking revenge for Dane.

Chapter Fifteen

Water. Dane stumbled down the mountain trail, following the distant sound of running water. Dizzy and weak from the fever and blood loss, he wandered into the forest clearing with only the light of the moon to guide his way. There, not more than twenty feet ahead, he spotted the shallow stream. Finally, he'd found the source.

Relief filled him with hope. Even with his tongue swollen tightly inside his dry mouth, he could almost smell the fresh mountain water. Maybe he would survive, after all. Today, before he heard the rushing water, he wouldn't have bet on it. Deep in the Colorado Rockies, he'd spent last night, after the wolf pack attack, lost.

Dane's mind fought back the memory of the vicious attack through a red haze of anger. The knot in his stomach grew tighter, and he balled his hands into fists.

Rourke's fate weighed heavily on him. Surely by now, his brother could be dead. As it was, his own injuries were serious, and he needed water badly. What little life still burned within him seemed like a mere ember as he dragged himself toward the stream.

Dehydration and the poison from his wounds made him wonder if this stream was merely another hallucination like the last one had been. The crimson stains on his hands and the blood running down the front of his shirt proved he hadn't imagined the entire incident, but that was where he drew the line. He couldn't wrap his mind around the fact that he'd been attacked by wolves the size of large bears with the eyes of men despite what Lindsey had shared with him or the DNA tests. The equally preposterous likelihood that a white unicorn had chased off the wolf had him believing he'd hallucinated it all except…

One reality remained. The gash on his left shoulder throbbed where the wolves' bites had torn the flesh away. The burning pain spread through him like a brand, spreading toxins minute by minute. The gnawing fever that had started earlier racked his body with white-hot chills. So when he saw the creek, he began to believe he might survive, after all. That was before the effects of the bite escalated making his bones ache and his muscles violently spasm. Shortly after he envisioned his hands turn into claws, he began to lose hope.

Exhausted, Dane dropped to all fours, crawled to the water's edge, and rolled in. He groaned with relief. *Ah, the water is no mirage.*

Too weak to move any farther, he flopped to his back in the shallows. *So cool.* The water should have been more of a relief to his hot body. He imagined steam rising off him, yet nothing eased the flames burning him alive.

The moon, almost full overhead, grew fuller, and the fever pitch within him increased along with his throbbing misery. The spasms in his aching muscles became even fiercer than before. The torture intensified to a new level.

Tired of fighting, his moans turned to tormented

screams, and he couldn't stop thrashing about, tossing his head from side to side. He was being wrenched apart limb from limb, physically enduring the dislocation of every joint in his body.

Wondering how much more he could take, he gave in to the pain and shrieked out in agony. Even to him, the noise he made came closer to the howls of an animal in pain than to the cries of a human.

As his vision darkened, he prayed for the capacity to pass out. Pain only existed in awareness. Hope existed in oblivion or death. Those options provided the escape he craved from the clutch of this raging affliction. But he couldn't manage to succumb. He remained conscious, and the pain went on and on with no end in sight. It seemed there'd be no escape for him as the convulsions became intolerable.

The last of the suffering rippled through him as he looked up at the moon. His vision grew dim and faded. His last thought before finally passing out was that dying would be a relief.

****

No pain. In fact, Dane felt so fantastic he assumed the rest had been a terrible nightmare.

He blinked to clear his vision and chanced opening his eyes. The moon shone brightly to the east of the tree line. An intelligent set of blue eyes stared back at him from within a white, furred face.

Wolf! He didn't move.

A cool, wet nose nudged his chin. No, his jaw. And the white wolf staring at him whined.

He decided he must be dead yet noted that the clear, slanted eyes staring steadily into his own held questions. Probably no more than his did. He suspected the fever had affected his thinking, especially when he looked at his hands.

No, paws.

Apparently he had died, and then he must have been resurrected as a large, black wolf.

Okay, I get it.

He let out a slow sigh of relief. At least this time, there wasn't anything left of the mind-numbing pain.

All this was improbable. *Preposterous.* He didn't even trust his eyes, especially when, to make matters worse, the white wolf staring at him shimmered like spun glass. She assumed the form of a woman. And then he recognized her. Lindsey.

As ridiculous as everything she had told him earlier sounded, a small part of him hoped her story was true. That she was real and she was for him.

When he drank in her beauty, the one woman Dane wanted heart and soul admittedly wanted him, too, in spite of the fact that his brother had claimed her as his and refused to share her. Her presence confirmed his brother was wrong. That same woman, stood before him naked, tempting, and perfect in every way. Her porcelain white skin shone practically iridescent under the moon. Long, pale blonde hair draped modestly around her slight shoulders and wrapped around her waist, hanging well past her hips.

In his fevered state, he couldn't help from thinking, *Exquisite.*

"Thank you." The woman's whispered words sounded in his head. *"But you aren't mad or dead. And I'm afraid, as absurd as all this seems, you're not hallucinating, either."*

Had she suspected his doubts?

"Yes, this isn't the first time we've been in each other's minds." She grinned a knowing smile. *"You're reading my mind, aren't you?"*

"I must be, since I'm unable to speak." Dane rose on all fours and shook. He checked himself over. *"I'm a wol—"*

"Yes, you are wolf-shifter. Things have become more complicated under the circumstances."

The pounding whoosh in his ears was the sound of his own heartbeat. When he tried to speak, the low rumbling coming from his chest resembled a growl. What was a man supposed to think when all his concrete beliefs imploded?

Wolf?

That thought should have bothered him more than it did, but somehow, during this transformation, his body had healed, and he felt stronger than ever before. Looking around, he studied the dark forest and found he could see into its depths as never before. The night looked different, sounded different, smelled...

He sniffed the air. He was different. His senses were heightened. Sharper. Clearer. More defined. Scents he'd never really identified before were suddenly recognizable.

Starting with her, for one.

His male body quickened, and he experienced a pang of guilt. Before the attack, Dane's single purpose focused on finding his brother if he'd survived. Something had drawn them to Enchanted Mountain, and he suspected it's what also brought about all this.

Dane felt the change begin, shifting him back to human form as he openly stalked his brother's woman. After his wolf's body compressed, crunching painfully back into his human form, he mentally asked, *"Will I ever change as easily as you?"*

"Yes, soon, it will be second nature," she answered. "Painless and thrilling."

In spite of the discomfort shifting back and forth caused him at the moment, he sensed more than noticed he was the same and yet different. Somehow more aggressive, more alive, more aware.

Another thing he realized was that shifting had another downside.

He was as naked as she and fully aroused by her presence. All he could think about was how badly he desired her, how much he'd wanted her from the first time he'd seen her. And hell, at the moment, he was so damn desperate his balls ached.

"I've been looking for you since last night. *I am for you.*" Her voice and her words wove a net around his heart. And despite how his groin tightened and heated, almost distracting his thoughts, he felt trapped.

Rourke will kill me for this.

The pressure building in the organ growing between his legs had him too busy physically responding to care about anything except his need. He slowly approached her instead of wondering what the hell the implication of her words meant to him or about shape-shifting into a wolf or why he was breaking the rule about coveting his brother's…what? Wolf, girlfriend, mate?

Those last few words of hers imprinted in his mind. They concerned him most. She'd said, *"I am for you."*

Her words angered him. What did it mean? She'd said it before. He'd heard her when she said that to Rourke, too. He wondered why she had said that same vow to Rourke just yesterday if she were meant for him. Last night? How much time had passed while he'd gone through this change?

He panicked. "What happened to Rourke?"

****

Lindsey's heart flipped. Dane's eyes flashed, and his lips pulled back in a snarl. His human face turned almost feral. Even though he clearly didn't understand what was happening to him, the expression on his face proved one thing—he'd adapt. The fight-or-flight response wasn't an issue with him. He'd do whatever was necessary. She could tell that by his wide-set stance and the grudging set of his shoulders.

The man looked as good naked as Lindsey had imagined and as capable as her succubus hoped his reputation implied. The dark wolf prince of the forest had finally returned, and if the old myths were true, he was hers. Convincing him to accept his rightful place as head of his pack wouldn't be easy, and making him understand he was part of their ménage might be harder. She was worried. The hard line of his jaw told her exactly how stubborn the man could be in any form, and two males unwilling to share one female was never a good situation.

She glanced up at the moon. It rose ever higher in the night sky. Time remained to ease his transition, yet the moon phase grew longer each night. Two nights left until the moon reached its full phase. Beltane approached, and the prophecy must be fulfilled.

The increasing tremor in his hands proved she would have to persuade him to take her soon. Apparently, he wouldn't give in to his primal instincts so easily. She could almost hear him thinking about

Rourke. Under the circumstances, Dane was too honorable for his own good.

His golden eyes flickered and then narrowed. His nostrils flared. While he stood still as stone watching her, she couldn't even tell if he was breathing. More than the tremor that shook his hands and racked his body, the telltale erection was the one sure thing that gave away his growing desire.

They didn't have time for his principles if she wanted to save his life. She'd seduce him if she must to convince him to mate with her. Before the moon reached its zenith, they still had to find Rourke, and the three had to bind before the full moon. His beast would run rampant on Beltane unless they were with him.

The rogue wolf who had attacked Dane wasn't an ordinary shifter. He'd turned Were sometime before the end of last year. Something about the group who ran with him was different, more dangerous. They were out of control, and his bite would be fatal unless she assisted Dane through his Were conversion.

Tears burned behind her closed lids, tears she refused to shed. She would never really be Dane's unless Rourke could accept their fate, and knowing Dane understood still hurt her. He knew she belonged to his brother first.

Rourke would be furious about this, but she didn't think he'd want his brother to die.

****

"Dane, I *am* for you."

"No, you're not. I heard you say that to him. What have you done to us?"

"I did nothing. *He* bound us with his words without understanding what he was doing. Without knowing.

147

Before I could explain."

Dane inspected her, from her well-muscled body to her full, shapely breasts. If this female was his reward for suffering through the painful transition of the full moon once a month, it would almost be worth risking Rourke's wrath.

When she blinked, her thick, dark lashes fanned a shadow beneath her eyes. The action seemed almost reticent. At once both shy and damn sexy. He got the sense she awaited his approval. Could she doubt any man would want her?

Besides, denying his desire with his cock standing at full attention seemed useless.

At the moment, Dane didn't care who she was or what she meant. He didn't care that his brother had forbidden him to consider her. Suddenly, this was a perfect case of the little head—well, not so little at the moment—ruling the big head.

A quick smile formed on her soft, pillowed lips, as if she'd heard his thoughts. Damn, he'd have to watch that in the future. And he would, just as soon as he could stop thinking about her mouth.

He tore his attention away from her flawless lips and met her perfect, silver-blue eyes, all big, rounded, and innocent. The hopeful stare she turned back on him made something possessive rise inside him.

"You are so beautiful." The timbre of his voice sounded deeper than usual, raspy and hoarse, thick with arousal. A great deal of residual wolf must have remained in him, because he was feeling more beast than man at the moment. As she approached him, apparently unconcerned that his cock stood erect, hard, and ready, he was practically growling out his words.

"You were attacked by the rogue Were. You must mate immediately after the attack to prevent the Were virus from turning you rogue. Only mated Weres are tolerated. Rogues are hunted to their death." Her husky voice sounded unbelievably sexy, turning him inside out. "Your need is great."

"Thanks for noticing." He followed her glance down to his erection. "Are you offering your services?"

"If you'll have me. Your need is greatest right now, especially with the moon approaching its zenith. I am for you."

If he'd have her? He closed his eyes and sniffed. "I can smell your arousal." His cock bobbed against his belly, and his balls tightened. Had he ever been this hard? This desperate? "What about Rourke?"

Her eyes filled with tears. "He wouldn't want to lose you to the dark, to death."

"Death?"

"Yes, without me to help you through the night, you will be hunted. The Other will hunt you. You will die."

"I guess that should make this easier. Fuck you and betray my brother, or die."

When the breeze blew a strand of his hair into his face, he combed it back from his forehead to get an unimpeded view of her. The breeze rustled her hair as well, and her nipples tightened into pale pink berries, poking through strands of her long, blonde curls. He licked his lips, imagining the sensation of taking them into his mouth and sucking.

Mine. Mate. Forever. The words filled his head.

The sight and scent of her made his gut hurt and his groin ache with greater need. Fighting his arousal seemed like a useless effort. The adrenaline surged, pumping blood through him, and his mounting desire almost frightened him.

She was aroused, but she didn't seem all that enthusiastic. Willing but doing her duty? This wasn't how he wanted her, but with his growing need, he didn't think he'd be able to stop.

"I don't want to take you against your will, but know this. I am going to fuck you if you don't run now. Something's happening, and I won't have the control to stop if you ask me. So run now if you want to get away." His harsh words came out like a promise more than a threat, and he couldn't keep himself from moving toward her. Stalking her.

"You would catch me even if I ran. That is the way of it. Dane, I am for you, too."

Too? Then he heard her words of acceptance.

"Yours. Mate. Forever."

His humanity bordered dangerously close to the shattering point.

She hadn't retreated as he neared and then towered over her, body to body. Before he realized he'd even moved, he wrapped an arm around her small waist. Dragging her toward him, he pulled her against his chest, slamming her body against his. He inhaled her fragrance and sighed. He was suddenly as fast as she implied.

With his naked body painted against her perfect skin, he relaxed. He was surprised when she cupped his face in her tiny hands and brought her lips up to softly kiss his.

"I understand," she murmured. "I'm here to help you through your transition."

Something in him needed more, demanded more, wanted everything. He whispered through tight lips, "Just through transition?"

She nuzzled his neck. "What will be will be."

But her gentle submission didn't soothe him. Instead, her compliance compelled the beast to rise within him and surge to the surface. "I'm warning you. This *thing* inside me…well, I'm not in control."

"I know."

"I can't guarantee what I'll do. I don't know if you'll be safe or that I won't harm you." He tried to find some way to warn her that despite looking entirely human, the beast ruled his body.

Her laughter bubbled out of her, a musical, tinkling sound that relaxed his fear. "*You could never harm me. I am for you.*"

The beast rose, almost burying Dane's fragile human nature beneath years of wild animal instinct. He seized her by the wrists and turned her around in his arms and then cupped her breasts in his hands. He nuzzled her neck, fighting the urge to bite down and drive his cock into her without prelude.

He held back, determined not to let the monster dominate his moment with her, not until he was as certain as she was that he couldn't hurt her.

The softness of her skin overwhelmed him, and desire sent the old, familiar tightness rippling up his spine and tightening his balls when his cock slipped between the twin mounds of her ass. He pressed against her damp folds in an attempt to ease the growing pressure, never remembering being this mindless with arousal before. It was all he could do to prevent himself from throwing her to the ground and fucking her

E.L. March

without preparing her to take his new size or his aggressive animal nature.

Then he remembered she'd handled Rourke just fine. The beast inside him roared with pain and jealousy.

When he noticed the pulse beat at the base of her neck, an insatiable longing rose within him. Lust and desire and craving filled him. For what? He wasn't entirely sure, but he felt driven like a madman.

He sniffed her, licked her translucent skin, and explored the damp slit between her thighs with his fingers. The gush of warm liquid at his touch rewarded him and increased the tension in every muscle in his body.

That new familiar sound, like a low growl, resonated in his chest.

Her scent—pine woods, field flowers, and woman—filled his senses. The unruly lust, the bond he felt with her, the need to bury himself deep inside her and stay there forever were all new emotions. And this aggression? Well, that was a totally foreign element to his personality. What man didn't admit to testosterone highs from time to time? But he'd always been level-headed and had never acted on his aggressive nature. He'd been competitive, but even if his values hadn't changed, his approach sure had.

Under the circumstances, did he believe the mountain lived up to its name? *Enchanted.* Damn straight he did. Because he was going to fuck her, even knowing in doing so he'd be sealing his unknown fate.

Something told him the minute he entered her, he'd be damned. The only woman he'd ever really wanted had come to him as a white wolf and claimed she was for him after having been with his brother.

Dane had always prided himself on his ability to control his emotions. With her, the ability melted away like a snowflake in summer. He contemplated the woman he had to fuck right now or die from wanting or fever. Did it matter which?

Lindsey belonged to Rourke, yet she seemed more vital to his survival than food or water or air. She would be his undoing. No one liked being helpless against his own desires, and this was a classic case of impotence on an entirely different level.

As his dick got harder, his brain quit rationalizing. Even if he could stop himself, his beast wouldn't let him, and for a moment, he thought Lindsey had something to do with it.

He extended his tongue, tasting the salt on her neck, and she turned her cheek in response to him. Touching her lips to his, her sweet fragrance, the scent inundating him, encouraged him to deepen the kiss. An energy surrounded them, one of heat and light. He felt like he was drowning in her life force, and yet he couldn't release her.

Mine.

The beast rose higher and pushed Dane brutally as he fought to slow down. It was damn near impossible to resist the urge to push her to her knees and take her from behind, especially when she rubbed her ass against his groin and gave off that special scent that made him brainless. The battle was lost when she whimpered and dropped to her knees, spreading her thighs wide, waiting. His damn cock looked like a divining rod searching for water as he took his place on his knees behind her. She moaned and arched into the hand he placed between her damp folds to gauge if and how ready she was. Her short, blonde curls were wet, her entrance slick and slippery with her juices.

He had to taste her first, had to bury his face in her pussy and lap at her honey until she screamed his name. His name.

"Say *my* name, Lindsey."

He rubbed her nub and licked her pussy lips, sucking the liquid cream from her core until she writhed, moaning and begging him to take her.

"Penetrate me now. Please enter me. Complete me. Finish this, I beg you."

He used his hands on her breasts and pulled his tongue out of her and growled. "Say *my* name."

"Please, fill me— What did you say?"

"Say my name! I want to be sure you know who's fucking you this time, Lindsey, and when you come, it better be my name you shout."

"Dane." Her voice sounded like smooth brandy when she whispered his name.

"Say it again."

"I know exactly who's pleasuring me at the moment, Dane. And when I climax, you can be assured it will be your name on my lips." Her hair wrapped around him. The magical tendrils stroked him reassuringly, pulling him to her.

When he tested her tight opening with a single finger, she exhaled and gasped. He looked down at his enormous erection and shook his head. *Where the hell did this cock come from?* There was no way his new girth or length was going to fit into her tight channel without a struggle and a great deal of pain on her part. "I don't want to hurt you."

"Dane, all will be fine. I'm part succubus, made for sex."

Succubus? He was a shifter, a wolf. So was she, and God only knew what Rourke was. He'd think later.

He closed his eyes and pressed his long, hard length against her cleft, patiently letting her prepare for the invasion. This was the miracle he had prayed for. Her pussy was as tight as a virgin's, yet she wasn't, and her succubus blood warned him she wouldn't respond like any woman he'd ever come across. She was hot and ready, as desperate for fucking as a cat in heat.

Where were his options? *Oh, damn.* Life had turned upside down.

She turned halfway around and stroked his cock just the way he liked to be touched, fondling his balls almost like she understood the pleasure he derived from it. There was no holding back, not anymore, no more choices. He was going to fuck a shifter who was part succubus, and if he survived, his brother would certainly kill him. Why? Because the woman was his.

Rourke?

Dane's cock thickened. Guilty thoughts didn't stop him.

He massaged her entrance, stimulating her swollen clit before he plunged his fingers into her white-hot heat. *Mine.* His other hand caressed the soft skin of her breast, the pleasure forcing a sigh from her lips and his. Her skin was so tempting, so silky he couldn't resist kissing the pulse at her neck as he tweaked her nipple, all the while knowing the smile forming on his lips was as sardonic as the situation he was in.

He shook off his thoughts as her thick honey dripped over his hand. His gut clenched with need and shame. Only one other man had ever been inside her, and that knowledge tore him apart. Once he finished satisfying this lust for his brother's woman, he'd have to figure out how to distance himself from their strange attachment. Then he had to get out of here and as far away from the mountain as possible. Because if he stayed, he knew one thing was certain. He'd take her again, no matter the consequences.

Rourke would kill him for touching her, and if he didn't, Dane knew that threat wasn't going to be enough to stop him. Not now. Nothing was. He was going to fuck her anyway. The outcome was inevitable.

"Dane, this is right. This is meant to be. We'll make everything work, you'll see." Lindsey's voice entranced him. He wished she'd keep talking and shut out the warnings in his head.

The moon rose higher in the sky, and his blood felt like fire boiling inside him as he poised at her entrance. His demon rose inside him, threatening. This was more than the wolf. "What's happening?" he asked, panic filling him.

"Hurry, Dane, it's the Were madness. Don't succumb before you're inside me. I can help you control the insanity."

The adrenaline pumped up his control. "Say my name, damn it!"

"Fuck me now, Dane."

His brain exploded. His cock needed just one stroke, just this first stroke. He slid into her tight sheath, and as her pussy swallowed his throbbing cock, he damned himself. His beast needed more. He took the second stroke and the third and…

The panic waned, and the beast retreated, but the

mindless desire for her didn't stop. Paradise, all warm and moist, tight and receptive. Her sheath wrapped around his cock and sucked him, clenching around him in spasms as he pumped, thrust, and pounded his desire into her.

"Dane!" She shouted his name when she climaxed.

Her orgasm brought on his, but instead of the satisfaction he'd expected, something stabbed at his heart and his vision blurred. Her skin felt damp and tasted salty against his cheeks where he rested them on her back.

Sorry, Rourke.

If Rourke still lived.

The minute his brother saw him, he'd know. He'd know that he'd been—a loud scream bellowed through the night sky—betrayed.

Betrayer.

Dane shuddered.

Chapter Sixteen

Lindsey turned around in his arms and pulled him to her breast. When she felt the dampness against her breast, she wiped his face and gently touching her lips to his eyes, asked softly, "Dane, are you okay?"

He looked grim, not like a man who had just given her so much pleasure she felt boneless.

"Sure, great. I just discovered I'm a Werewolf, and I fucked my brother's girlfriend. I'm just peachy."

"You don't understand."

"Damn straight I don't understand. I don't understand how he could have been taken in by the likes of you! You *are* a succubus. You did something to make him crazy for you, like you've done to me."

"I did nothing, gave nothing to him or to you that you didn't take willingly. We are all bound. This experience with you was necessary."

"What? Necessary for who? Me? Shit! Tell me this wasn't a pity fuck."

"Oh, my God. Did it feel like a pity fuck to you? I told you. We are meant to be together, too. Rourke and I. You and I. All of us. I don't have all the answers yet. Even *I* don't understand what's going on. For some reason, fate bound me to both of you. But what's more important is we have to find Rourke before the moon wanes."

"Is he alive?"

"Yes, he must be, or I would know something happened to him. I can feel him."

"He can feel you, too. Can't he?"

When Lindsey didn't answer, Dane groaned. "Hell, I hope he didn't feel what you did a few minutes ago. Shit! He is going to kill me."

There was a loud flapping sound and a screech in the distance. Lindsey whipped around to see where the sound was coming from. "What was that noise?"

"It sounded like a huge bird of prey."

The enormous shadow passed over them, and when Lindsey saw what it was, she cringed. "Oh, no. It's Rourke." She tugged a reluctant Dane into the woods, intending to follow the dragon's course. "If he already shifted into the dragon, something must be terribly wrong. We have to get to him."

Dane pulled her up against him by the arm and didn't budge. "Let me get this straight." He stared up into the night sky, and a look of total bewilderment filled his expression. "I'm a wolf-shifter, and Rourke is a dragon? I thought he was a wolf-shifter, too."

She tugged him, but he stood still, waiting for an answer. "Some of us can take many forms. You were born a wolf-shifter, and now that you've been infected by the Were virus, you will shift into the Were form of the wolf at each seasonal full moon. Bound Weres are stable, but rogue Weres can be dangerous. That's why I am for you. Bonding with me saved you from going rogue and being hunted as a danger to the Others."

"So, now you are the light to my dark side, I take it?"

"You could say that." She coaxed him toward the path again.

159

He relented and moved with her, shaking his coal-black hair. "Hell, a dragon. Wouldn't you just know he'd one-up me?"

"Dane, this is really serious. We have to find him."

"I am serious. Where do we look?"

"When we get close enough, I can sense him. We exchanged blood." That made her wonder. Would she be able to shift into a dragon form? That might be helpful right now. "He's about a mile up ahead hunting the rogue Werewolf, the one you escaped from. We can travel faster if we shift."

"Then let's do it." He wasn't looking forward to the pain. "How?"

She smiled. "Focus on me. I'll help you through it, and don't worry about anything. You won't shimmer into your wolf, but it won't be as painful this time."

Dane tried to think "wolf" and focused on Lindsey. She shimmered into the white wolf again while he watched. She shifted so effortlessly he couldn't help being impressed, especially after his last experience.

He felt his temperature rise and his skin tingle. This time, as his bones elongated, he stared into Lindsey's pale blue eyes and heard her calming voice. *"Think about the wolf's form, sleek and muscular, strong and powerful. That's it. You're doing fine."*

His vision grew sharper, and he realized the shift was complete. *"Fast, simple, almost painless. Thanks."*

He shook himself and tested his balance by taking a step. *Cool!*

Lindsey's face looked like she smiled as he stalked around her. He heard her think, *"Let's find Rourke. Follow me."*

"Lead on, darlin'. I'm right behind you. By the

way, nice tail."

"Behave. Get serious."

"I am."

"Think dragon fight."

"I'm not fighting him, Lindsey."

"No, you're right. We could be saving him. He's inexperienced and fighting the Were alone."

Dane heard the commotion up ahead and mentally encouraged Lindsey to pick up her speed.

As they rounded the clearing, Dane saw Rourke. *"Holy shit."* The dragon was awesome.

"Wow!" Even Lindsey stopped dead in her tracks.

"He's enormous. Those wolf dudes are crazy to mess with him."

"Ah, those wolf dudes are friends of the Were who attacked you. Rourke smells your blood on them, and I think he's trying to avenge your death."

"Ironic. I'm not dead yet, but I will be when he finds out what we've done." Really, if he could have grinned, he would have.

All his male wolf testosterone pumped like rocket fuel through his system.

"Up for a fight?"

"You know it." He'd love to get his hands on the guys who attacked him. Now, he'd settle for getting his claws on them and some great big teeth.

Anger and the thought of revenge welled up inside him. The beast in him fought its way to the surface, all powerful and dangerous. Whoa, it felt good. He tried to hold the powerful beast back, but he couldn't stop his deeper urges to test his limits and let the shift happen. The Were in him was loose.

Hell, once he felt the beast's true essence, he

wondered if he could control it.

The other wolf had already shifted into his Were form, responding to the danger Rourke posed. He grew bigger and larger, a good match for Dane's Were, but Rourke's dragon held the trump card with his size alone.

Three more wolves came out of the cave and shifted. Four rogue Weres against Rourke and his Were? The rogue Weres were obvious by their flame-red eyes, like demon spawn. He hoped his eyes hadn't been affected like that. Red wasn't his best color. Then he remembered Lindsey had saved him from this insanity with their bond.

He wasn't sure about the odds, but he doubted it was an even fight.

He circled in front of Lindsey just in case she proved to be their one weak link. If Dane didn't know with some inner instinct that she'd been holding out on them, he'd have been worried. So when her transformation began, he let out a sigh of relief.

She started her shift from her wolf with that dazzling shimmer, and the light around her grew larger and brighter.

All the opponents watched, amazed.

He was right. She had been holding out.

When the astounding display ended, the mist cleared, and a white dragon stood beside him. She matched Rourke's enormous size, head to tail.

"Nice going, Lindsey! Okay, now let's help Rourke avenge me. Tell him to save one for me. Those bastards worked me over good."

"Wait, Dane, let me talk to Rourke first."

She turned her mind on the giant, ebony dragon.

"I'm here, Rourke. Dane is alive. He's safe, but he's turned. He's over there in the form of the black Werewolf. Let us help you fight the rogues and the Weres."

Rourke lifted his massive head to the sky, and with a roar so loud Dane could barely stand it, he attacked the Weres. Dane picked out one from the bunch and went after him. Within minutes, the battle ended with the corpses of four dead Weres at their feet. Lindsey roared out a flame and disintegrated the mess with one simple breath.

Dane was impressed. *"Tidy clean-up."*

"Thank you."

She shimmered back into her human form, if one could call her dazzling form human. She looked like no other human female he had ever seen, radiant and perfect, far more of everything than he could describe.

Rourke stared down at her. His emotions had him trapped in his dragon body. When he bent his huge head to nuzzle her, her hair swept up around his large neck and caressed the dragon as she whispered to him in a comforting tone and patted his muzzle.

Rourke lifted his broad head and bellowed into the night sky.

Dane shrank into his human form without even noticing the shift this time. He stepped back into the bushes, waiting for her to soothe the beast, and when he glanced over at her, he looked for reassurance. "Is everything all right?"

"He smells you on me."

"Great, I'm a dead man."

"I have to encourage him to shift back. Once I do, he'll be able to see the reasons in my mind."

"Oh, okay. Like that's going to calm him down. He'll be all forgiving when he *sees* me fucking the one woman he gave me strict orders not to touch."

Rourke belched fire in the sky, and Dane took refuge deeper in the trees. "Yup, I'm a dead man."

"Dane, there were extenuating circumstances. He wouldn't have wanted you to die. He loves you."

"Tell *him* that. Can't you get him to stop that infernal racket?"

"He's feeling betrayed."

Rourke roared again, and flames shot higher into the night sky.

"No shit!"

"He's hurting, and he can't understand the reasons why we had to do what we did. Let me convince him to shift. His beast won't understand reasoning, but the man will."

"You don't know Rourke as well as I do. He won't be much more understanding about this than his dragon is."

Flames filled the night sky again and again as Lindsey stood between Rourke and Dane.

"Do whatever you think is right, then, and hurry, before he charcoal broils me."

She called to Rourke. *"Shift back, Rourke. Come to us."*

The black dragon let out a scream, and a dark cloud of smoke rose in the air. After it settled, Rourke stood magnificent and naked before them.

His scowl reflected the emotions Lindsey sensed.

Lindsey wrapped herself around Rourke and tried to explain why he smelled Dane on her.

"You better talk him out of killing me—fast."

"Rourke listen—understand. Dane was dying. He would have died if he hadn't shifted. If I hadn't…saved him. Everything—destiny—fate would have been denied."

There was no denying that Dane felt a connection with Rourke through his connection with Lindsey. He was beginning to wonder where his thoughts stopped and theirs started. Their psychic attachment grew stronger with each passing minute.

"Rourke, what's going on with us?" Dane knew his brother felt this, too.

Rourke turned his back to both of them, unwilling or unable to answer.

"I want more," she said, "crave more, more of the emotional connection between us, the rich mental bond as well as the sexual one with both of you. Do you feel it calling to you, too?"

"Fuck, yes!" Rourke whipped around and faced her. "Minus the sexual attraction to Dane. Yeah, I do."

She put her hands on her hips, exhaled, and frowned at Rourke, and Dane stepped up. "Shit, Rourke, I got the point. It's not like I'm panting for you, either. You don't have to keep repeating yourself. I'm clear on that point. You don't do guys."

"Just so you understand where I'm coming from, bro. Your hairy ass just doesn't turn me on."

Lindsey laughed. "I know both of your deepest feelings, and Rourke, let me assure you, this will be different when the time comes."

"Fine. I'm not promising anything." Rourke snorted.

Chapter Seventeen

By the time all three wolves returned to the lodge and shifted back into human form, they were in agreement on one thing. They'd relax and talk through the facts as they saw them. Rourke decided they'd meet back in Lindsey's room because it opened to the hot tub deck.

As usual, Dane analyzed everything scientifically while Rourke looked for a solution. Holding out for something reasonable, something tangible in a reality gone haywire, Dane joined Rourke's refusal to accept their fate without question. Tonight, Rourke's approach leaned toward denial, as ludicrous as that seemed after recent events.

Lindsey was the only one of the three who seemed resigned to their future. She announced she was going to soak in the hot tub and relax. "This is perfect, very relaxing." She moaned as she sank down in the bubbling water. "You should both join me."

"In there with you? Relaxing? No, I don't think so." Rourke sulked on a lounge chair with a bottle of beer poised at his lips, never turning away from her. "Later."

"Uh, me, too." Dane couldn't take his eyes off her naked body, either. The hot tub didn't hide her assets from him. "Maybe later. Right now, I want to think clearly."

Rourke did turn away then, just long enough to glare at him. "Well, if you really want to think clearly, maybe you should stop staring at her like she's the main course."

Dane moved and sprawled in the chair ten feet away from either of them. Rourke was right. After his seething glance, Dane decided to keep his distance from everyone. He wasn't sure what his body wanted. He read what Rourke's wanted in his expression. Sex? Definitely. Blood, flesh, violence? Perhaps.

Staring at the empty glass of wine tilted dejectedly in his hand, he refilled it, took a long sip, and then put the uncorked bottle down beside him on the deck.

He glanced over at Rourke and wondered what facts Lindsey had kept from them. Without thinking, he leaned forward in his chair, and a question spilled out of him. "Lindsey, do you know who Rourke's biological father is?"

"No, but Aryan, the dragon-shifter, is the most likely one to have sired him. There hasn't been a pure dragon-shifter around Enchanted Mountain in a thousand years, and none at all since Aryan was banned."

"Can't you put on that bathing suit thingy you had on the other day?" Rourke fidgeted in his chair with a towel over his hips and grimaced when he looked at her.

"Don't be ridiculous. What with all the shifting we've been doing recently, and everything else, clothes just get in the way."

"I'm not being ridiculous. I'm hard. Dane can't concentrate with you naked in front of him. Look at him. No, don't. His cock is at full mast."

"I'm fine with his cock." Lindsey smiled at Dane.

Dane smiled back, stopping when Rourke grumbled under his breath.

Dane shrugged. "No, really, it's okay. I'm not having a problem."

Rourke shook his head. "I doubt that. All the blood drained out of your head when she shifted back."

"Could be, but we should probably get used to this, this being naked together under all circumstances," Dane said.

"Let's just say I'm not convinced you can concentrate and leave it at that," Rourke snapped back.

The dirty look he gave Dane turned deadly when he caught him glancing at Lindsey's breasts again. Then a rumble of angry growls rippled out of Rourke and resounded like a restrained warning.

Dane shrugged. "Okay, I admit it. Maybe we'll need a little more time to get used to this arrangement." He ran a hand over his erect cock and got up. Turning his back to the others, he walked to the gate, focusing his attention away from Lindsey's bobbing breasts. He figured it was safer to concentrate on the surrounding landscape. "The mountain is…really big."

Great, couldn't he have come up with a more pertinent comment? He didn't have to turn around to tell what they were thinking. He felt their eyes boring into his back. Sure enough, when he turned around, both Rourke and Lindsey looked incredulous.

"Ah, have you finally lost it?" Rourke asked.

"That's a real conversation starter." Lindsey followed the dry comment with a smile then didn't bother to repress a giggle.

They all seemed to relax a little. Even Rourke's

shoulders shook with amusement when Dane said, "Well, it is big. And pretty damn impressive, with the mist swirling around the summit."

He was determined to get out of this mess without looking like a complete ass.

"Usually if there's mist on the mountain," she said, "it's caused by magic. Someone or something has conjured it to screen their presence."

"Shit, you're kidding, right?"

"Could Aryan be hiding up there, right now?" Rourke asked.

"No, not Aryan. He might return, but he isn't here yet. He's not stable enough to hide. At one time he was the most powerful and one of the most lethal killers of all shifters before he was banished."

"If he was so bad, I'd like to meet the one who had the power to banish him." Rourke sounded impressed.

Lindsey turned and gave him a small sad smile. "In a way, you did, Rourke. Your mother banished him."

"His mother banished her mate? The dragon?"

"Yes. Only a bonded mate can banish. She went to the Council and requested the fae to devise a magical force field to keep Aryan out. Until he realizes the field no longer stands since her death, he can't enter the lands of the Lore."

"Why wouldn't he try coming back before now?"

"Sarah's life span should have exceeded her short thirty years."

"Was it his demon blood that drove him insane?"

"In a way. Dragon-shifters with demon blood usually bond with two mates. Aryan refused to bond with any other besides Sarah. That's why he was so uncontrollable. He refused his other bonded mate. No one knows who it was or why he wouldn't accept the bond, but now, I suspect it was Rafe."

"What happened?"

"Everything was fine until he turned dragon. Then Aryan went berserk and murdered first one human for her flesh and then a fae for her blood. He didn't stop killing until Sarah put a stop to the massacres the only way she knew how. She rejected him. After binding with him, banishing would have killed her if she hadn't been claimed immediately by Rafe. I bet she didn't know she was carrying Rourke when she turned to him for protection. It may have been why she asked Grayland to hide Rourke when she was dying, knowing Aryan could return after he discovered her death. The forest fae concealed her death until Rafe's death last year. Then without a leader, the news leaked out."

Dane thought of something. "Aryan's heritage was dragon mixed with demon, right?"

"Yes." Lindsey hesitated. "Why?"

"Just wondering. There was more in Rourke's DNA."

"Why didn't you tell me what you found?"

"I didn't know what I found, for God's sake. They don't have a category for dragon that I'm aware off."

"So you found demon DNA in Rourke's blood?"

Rourke's shoulders slumped, and he dropped his head to his hands. "What other kind of evil DNA is floating around in my genes?"

"DNA isn't evil. It's what you do with it that determines good or evil," Dane said.

Lindsey splashed water over her upper chest above her floating breasts. "Aryan is the purest dragon-shifter alive and has outlived all the rest. It's the demon blood in his background that makes him aggressive. Your demon DNA would be diluted with human and wolf-shifter DNA."

Rourke stood and began pacing. "I want to sort through all this. I need to run."

She shook her head. "Come here, Rourke."

He raised an eyebrow at her order but walked over to the hot tub anyway.

She held up a finger and waved him in closer to her. "Here. Right here." She touched her finger to her lip. "Kiss me."

"What?"

"You bound me to you, right?"

"I guess—"

"Then kiss me good-bye before you go, like a real husband." She puckered up.

Rourke let out a loud bark of laughter. "You sure know how to break a tense moment." He walked back to her and pulled her halfway out of the hot tub.

Dane watched the tension ease out of Rourke when his mouth grazed her cheek. The tension in the air visibly lifted when his lips touched hers. He kissed her softly at first, and then his mouth claimed hers possessively, and a tangle of tongues turned into an open-mouthed fuck. She looked pink and breathless when he released her, and the heat level in the air turned up several degrees.

"Wow!" she said.

Rourke shifted into the alpha wolf without so much as a tremor and headed for the gate. "*I need some space.*"

Dane let out a sigh as Rourke ran off into the star-filled night.

171

"Do you need company?" Lindsey shouted after him. "Or do you want some alone time?"

"Alone. I need to think."

"Whew!" Lindsey leaned back and relaxed. "That man is coiled tighter than a steel cable."

Dane rolled his head and loosened his own shoulders. His cock felt like steel and throbbed with desire, wanting to be buried inside her.

He needed a distraction. "Tell me more about his father before he gets back."

"For the last thirty years, Aryan's been raising hell all over the world with no one powerful enough to stop him."

"Do you think we can?" Dane asked.

"When Rourke shifts, we don't know how much of his human thought process he retains. You did say he has human DNA, right?"

Dane nodded. "Not much, but there's a human in his genetic woodpile somewhere."

"His dragon is larger and more deadly than any other shape-shifter beast alive in the Lore. I can't hold my dragon form for very long yet. Once you take enough of his blood, you may be able to shift into the dragon, too. Maybe not right away but eventually. When this Beltane comes and the moon eclipses, there won't be any power strong enough to control Rourke. Only his mates. Only us. We have to make sure we're all bound up nice and tight before then."

"Us? I don't understand. What *us* are you talking about?"

"According to legend, no one is safe from the dragon's bloodlust until he binds his mates to him. He bound me, and now he must bind you. Aryan raped and murdered humans, Lycans, and fae alike. Nothing would deter him, and he continued his killings every full moon when the seasons changed until he was banished. We don't want the same thing to happen to Rourke."

"Like all the males of the Lore, won't I be affected?"

She nodded. "Every seasonal full moon, you will turn Were, and Rourke will go through his shift and hunt as the dragon. Both of your beasts must be kept under control, and we can help each other at that time."

"What's your secret?"

"You know I'm a succubus. My mates keep me from taking the souls of the innocent in dreams. I, too, will be affected by the seasonal full moon."

"So what you're saying is we save each other from our inner monsters."

"Yes, I'm beginning to think Aryan is the danger the Legends warned about. The only way Aryan can be defeated is by a creature of equal strength. The Lore's numbers are dwindling. Each of us has the necessary genetics to control Rourke's dragon, my succubus, and your Were. Maybe the three of us can protect the mountain and the Lore from his sire."

"Okay, I think I understand the reasoning for all this. So what do we have to do?"

"Dane, it's not so much what we have to do, but apparently the rules have changed. The three of us have to complete the bond we started to form so we can lead our people. We represent the most important elements of our heritages."

"Like merging our DNA and our abilities with each other?"

"Yes, exactly. We'll share my fae magic, the demon strength, the dragon's stamina, the stealth of the wolf, and the Were's cunning."

"What about the succubus?" Dane asked. "How will we put that talent to use?"

"It'll help when we form the ménage bond. Once fully bound, our union will be permanent. Eternal. There's no changing our minds once we've made the commitment to each other and the Lore."

"Yeah, yeah, sounds great, but I sense there's something more I should know."

She was reluctant to answer. "You and Rourke have to complete your bond. You will take one another's blood during sex."

"Okay."

"Dane—"

"So, what's the problem? I didn't mind it. We exchanged blood when we had sex."

"Uh, that would be sex with each other."

"Like you, me, and Rourke?"

"No. Like *you* and Rourke. You and I are already bound, and Rourke and I are bound. That leaves only the two of you."

"You're kidding right?"

"This isn't a joking matter, Dane. If what I believe is true about Aryan being the threat to the prophecy, our very survival and the survival of the Lore depends on us being able to resolve our issues and form a complete ménage."

"You think Rourke and I— That's sick. We're brothers."

"No, actually, you're not. You, better than anyone, should know that."

174

"Oh, okay. Technically, you're right. We're not brothers—maybe very distant cousins, if that." He shook his head and turned her to face him. "Lindsey, honey, I don't think he'll ever agree to this."

"You would?

"I'm not sure."

"We'd all have to mate. Together, you, Rourke, and I have to share blood and sex to complete our union. The sharing of sex and blood between all three of us will create the eternal ménage bond."

"Ah, does Rourke understand this?"

"Not exactly. Not all the intimate details. But he's got the idea from my thoughts. I think he's leaving the final decision up to you."

"Great. How much time do we have?"

"Until the full moon wanes. By then, our bond must be completed."

Dane shook his head again and turned to walk away. He shifted like he'd been doing it all his life. He glanced toward the forest with renewed interest. *"Come. We have to find Rourke."*

Chapter Eighteen

Lindsey could barely keep up. Dane was coming into his own power. The two wolves raced through the tight woods, following Rourke's scent as he climbed higher up the mountain trail. Magic filled the air with the mist. She could feel Celia's mark on all this. What was she hiding?

Rourke turned his wolf's body, bunched his massive chest, and lowered his head into a defensive stance when he sensed their approach. It took a moment before he relaxed and lowered his guard.

"I've been wondering. This eternal union between the three of us—what exactly does it entail?" Rourke mentally asked Lindsey.

The wolf's amber eyes were a paler version of his human dark brown eyes. They were less disconcerting than the silver, swirling irises they turned to when he changed into the larger, more dangerous dragon.

"More of what you two have been doing over the years, from what I gather. Sharing women."

She glanced up into the sky and marked the moon's progress. They would see him turn into the beast again at the height of the full moon. She couldn't help but notice how Rourke's arrogant, suspicious disposition glared back at her from behind those eyes whether he was man or wolf or dragon.

"You?" He snorted.

"You've shared plenty of women so far. What's one more?"

Then she nuzzled Dane, hoping the reminder of how they'd been together in the past would make him feel more at ease with the knowledge he'd have to sexually submit to Rourke.

"We share women we don't care about. There's nothing at stake."

"Sorry, let me correct one important thing and make this one point perfectly clear. In the future, you will be sharing only one woman. Me." She rose and whipped her body around Rourke's, rubbing her scent all over him. *"If you didn't know it before, I'm warning you now—my succubus doesn't share."*

"Then there are two major differences," Rourke said.

"Really?"

"We'll be sharing you with no one else, either." Rourke shook his massive head and body. Dane followed suit. The men shifted back to their human forms so quickly Lindsey would have sworn they didn't even realize they'd done it.

"And the other thing?" she asked.

Dane stepped between them and interrupted. "Rourke and I have never purposely touched each other during our ménages. We've never, you know, been like that together."

"Okay, I understand, but you've also never made love to a succubus together, either." In a hushed voice, she asked Dane, "Can you honestly admit you've never wondered what being with a man would be like?"

"Will admitting my darkest fantasies affect our relationship?"

"No. Are you worried about your lifelong friendship with him surviving this admission?"

"Honestly? Yes."

"So you have fantasized about having sex with men?" Lindsey murmured into his ear.

"No, not men in general." Dane lowered his voice even more and admitted in a low whisper, "Actually, with Rourke, specifically."

"When?" Rourke's head shot up.

"You weren't supposed to hear that."

"Since all this, my sense of hearing has improved. Spit it out. When?"

"When we did Simone. And then again one other time when we did Michelle. Every once in a while when we've fucked some of those women together, you brushed your hand against me, or I accidently touched you. I wondered what it would feel like to really caress you." Dane looked away. "Sometimes I imagined your hands on me the way you touched them."

"Shit."

"Does it bother you?"

Rourke shrugged. "I don't know how it makes me feel. Surprised. Not really. I figured something like that crossed your mind when you left in the middle of our last three-way with Amelia."

"Well hell, it surprised me." Dane looked away again and talked to no one in particular. "I never thought I'd enjoy being dominated, and at the time, I just thought I was confused, aroused, caught up in the moment." He turned back and stared straight at Rourke. "You know, Rourke, when you get all dominant, you're pretty damn awesome. Imagining you dominating me the way you did those women made me harder than I've ever been."

"I didn't know you felt that way." Rourke sounded sympathetic, but his jaw clenched. A thoughtful expression crossed his face. "But there's another issue."

"What?"

"Don't go getting all girly on me—"

"Fuck you—"

"Yeah, wouldn't you just love that? Now don't go getting your feelings hurt, because you know I love you, Dane, and I wouldn't have a problem tying you up or spanking you, but more? I haven't ever given it a serious thought. You know, touching you that way. No offense."

"None taken. No problem, my ego isn't damaged." Dane waved his hand at Rourke. "I prefer the ladies anyway. As long as they keep lining up, I can live without your interest." He smiled, then frowned when he looked at Lindsey. "Except from now on, no more other women."

"This conversation is all unnecessary. I've already made my decision." Rourke set up a wall of determination in the air around him.

Dane stared. "Let me guess. You aren't up for sharing, I know."

"You're right. I'm not up for it, but I'm willing to share Lindsey this time with you under one condition. You have to agree to accept the submissive role in our relationship."

"You want me to bottom for you, Rourke? Is that it?" Dane's lips curled around the snarl, a low, menacing sound. "I didn't know my ass tempted you so much."

Rourke's eyes narrowed, and he growled a low

179

warning rumble in his chest. "Trust me. Like I said, your ass holds no interest at all for me. I want your vow of submission…in all things."

Dane paced side to side, never taking his eyes off Rourke. "Why does it have to be all one way? Your way?"

"You know why. I can't change my makeup. I need to dominate to come."

Lindsey interrupted them. *"Why don't we wait and see how we feel once we're involved before we start wrangling for positions?"*

Dane's head snapped around, and he glared back at Rourke. "Just promise one thing. You will share her equally with me."

Rourke turned narrowed eyes on Dane and frowned. A wave of jealous greed swept across his face, one Lindsey and Dane couldn't miss. It was obvious that every possessive instinct had Rourke's beast warring with the concept of sharing her.

"No, I can't promise anything," he finally admitted.

Lindsey calmly shifted. Now, the two men stalked naked around the mountain pond while she dipped her feet into the water and waited for them to stop posturing and come to terms with the inevitable.

"What about you? You haven't agreed. Can you promise to submit?" Rourke's eyes narrowed, and a low warning growl rumbled through his chest.

"Will I have a choice?" Dane grumbled.

"Do any of us? Should I risk losing you and her, along with my soul, to the dragon forever?"

Lindsey watched Rourke closely. He was having a hard time holding on to his humanity. The dragon's jealousy controlled him. His eyes kept changing color and shape. The fiery energy exuding from him transformed his skin to that exquisite, multi-colored, pearled luminescence. It was both beautiful and fearsome to watch him.

The tenor of his voice dropped to a gravelly-sounding rasp. His hand trembled when he pointed his finger at Dane and spit out, "Remember this, the next time you fuck her will be after you submit to me. Once I establish dominance over you physically, we can fuck her together. Then and only then, we'll see how I feel about sharing. If that doesn't work,"—Rourke jabbed the finger into Dane's chest—"the beasts inside us can fight it out."

Dane inhaled, expanding his chest against Rourke's touch, and took a step closer. His livid anger whipped through the air, a tangible thing, but he said nothing.

"You broke the trust, Dane, when you fucked her. I would have died before breaking our trust."

"I would have killed innocents. I would have become the thing you fear."

The unfathomable rage rose up in Dane's alpha wolf, and she expected the men to shift back into the wolves they were growling like and start fighting, tumbling into snarling balls of teeth and claws and fur. But although Dane looked like he was ready to knock the shit out of Rourke for putting the horror of it all into words that way, Dane held back. He was capable of being submissive to Rourke, after all.

Lindsey felt the toll it took on him to pull the wolf back and hang on to his control. She was surprised by his strength of character and his ability to fight back his beast.

Rourke didn't blink. "I'm trying to come to terms with this thing between us, but trust doesn't come easy when my life as I knew it is turned upside down. I'm not even *who* I thought I was, let alone *what* I thought I was."

Dane stuck his chin out and came almost nose to nose with Rourke and snarled through clenched teeth. "Sorry, Rourke, but we all just had a change of plans. Apparently we will share her or turn into monsters. Without each other, where's our choice here?"

Lindsey reinforced Dane's point. "Our destiny is together. Fate bound us all to one another. Surely, there's a reason and a solution."

The muscles in Rourke's jaw tensed. He ran a hand down his face and shook his head. "You're right. There's never been a choice, has there? We've been trapped in this situation with no way out since the day his father shot my mother. Maybe even before."

She wanted to touch him, needed to touch him. But she didn't dare while his skin shimmered and his body trembled. "Together, we're complete, three interconnected parts that can't function without each other." Lindsey tried reasoning with him, but he was still lost somewhere in his mind, fighting his beast for control. "I never wanted you to feel trapped. Love shouldn't be a prison." She blinked to keep the tears at bay.

"Don't, Lindsey. My anger isn't about you or Dane or our feelings toward each other. It's about having that choice to love taken away and made for us that's pissed me off. The why, the how, the damn intimate details of our sexual relationship are being dictated by fate."

Rourke turned on Dane again, his eyes swirling

with the dragon's quick-silver warning. "I'll agree to this on one condition. I will only share her with a submissive male, and I will never relinquish my dominant position or take part in a submissive role in any way." Rourke's face flashed a sign of the dragon's muzzle beneath the surface. "Is that clear?"

Lindsey pulled Dane back, but he managed to spit out his comment. "Pig-headed prick. I figured as much."

Rourke held his ground. "Will you accept the terms of this arrangement?"

Dane's jaw clenched, and his muscles flexed before he conceded to Rourke's demand. "Yes. No. I don't know. What's the alternative?" He stopped pacing. "I wish I could simply say yes. It would make everything easier, but hell, Rourke, it's not just the sex with you. What if you can't share her with me after all this? I don't know what will happen if I can't make love to her again."

Lindsey couldn't help with their issues. It wasn't even a matter of choosing between the men. Dane would literally have to offer himself to Rourke without a guarantee he'd be part of their union in the future. The one thing she could make clear was how she felt about Dane. "I'm not sure I can survive without Dane, too."

"There isn't any other choice, then, is there?" Rourke looked like an immoveable rock when he asked Lindsey for confirmation.

"No," she whispered before linking fingers with Dane, holding on to him to reassure him. "We are the dragon's mates, and he must take two mates from the realm to rule. He's too unstable otherwise. Dane, if you're not part of this, when he surfaces, he'll kill you anyway. He won't let you live now that you've taken my blood."

"Shit!" Rourke stared at Lindsey. "We're talking about a part of me killing a man I've loved as a brother all my life." His resolve crumbled when his eyes met hers. The emotions etched on his face were clear. She felt the same sense of fate and his devastation. His pain was hers. "What kind of monster is inside me that could do that?"

Dane shook his head. "This arguing is pointless. I agree, Rourke, to all your demands. I'll just have to trust you."

"Thank you, Dane. Thank you. I realize the sacrifice you're making by trusting me," Rourke acknowledged.

"Maybe this will help." Lindsey released her glamour, the air filled with pheromones, male and female, and for an instant, she knew the men could think about nothing but sex. "This ménage will have its upside, too."

Dane looked down at his erect cock. He'd hardened in a flash. "Okay, I get it. You've got that aspect covered. All I can think about is sex. Sex with you, sex with Rourke. Hell, the stump is even looking good. Stop it before I get splinters."

Rourke didn't escape the effects of her magic. He shifted in place uncomfortably, ran his hand over his erection, and cleared his raspy throat. "Is there anything else we should know about all this?" His expression was grim. He shrugged and rolled his neck to loosen the muscles visibly tightening there.

"Another positive is we'd be capable of being in each others' minds at will, experiencing each others' sensations."

"That could be good." Dane almost smiled at Rourke. "I could fly in your mind like the dragon."

"What's the downside, Lindsey?" Rourke asked.

"Other than the obvious, there'd be no turning back for any of us. I don't want to exist with you both in an eternity of resentment."

Dane's brow furrowed. "What else?"

"Honestly, I don't know what will happen once you and Rourke turn at the time of the next full moon, the Beltane moon. Dane, your Were may not be willing to be submissive to the dragon. If we can't establish our ménage by then, I'm afraid you'll try to kill each other over me."

"Shit, this gets worse by the minute."

"Or not. Maybe my Aunt Celia's right," Lindsey said. "What if this is our destiny? Maybe fate knows what's right for us."

"Even if I choose to submit to Rourke as a man and a wolf, are we sure my Were is going to cooperate?"

"Not if you have reservations going into this."

"As much as I want you, Lindsey, I have to be honest with myself for all our good. What happens then?"

"I don't think that will be a problem. Subconsciously, you've already been able to submit to his authority. He's probably the older brother. He acts like it, anyway. The CEO of your company, the bossy buddy." She smiled.

"Ah, hey. Wait just a minute—" Rourke tried to stop them.

"All too true." Dane grinned.

"Don't worry," she said. "My fae succubus and I

will be part of the process." Her voice turned into a low whisper, and she observed her effect on Dane. His lids lowered, and his breathing grew shallow when she sent the picture of the three of them into his mind. "You'll be so aroused by my fae nature, you'll not only be able to yield to his physical domination, you'll beg for it. I can guarantee you'll love our union."

"But will Rourke?"

"He's as susceptible as you are."

Dane pulled Lindsey against him and hugged her. The images had aroused him. With his cock pressed hard against her pussy and his mouth close to her ear, he whispered, "After only being with women all my life, I don't know."

"I can make it happen for you if that's what you're worried about. You will perform, Dane," she said.

Rourke ran his hands through his hair and let them drop to his side. His shoulders slumped. "I hate this. I won't risk hurting either of you." He tried to explain but without much enthusiasm.

Lindsey nuzzled Dane's neck and whispered in his ear, "Dane, you'll be fine, and so will Rourke."

"If my own personal succubus promises me nothing but endless pleasure, who am I to argue? Rourke, I'm okay with this if you are. I trust you."

"And I need you both," Lindsey said as she moved to embrace Rourke.

"I want you." Rourke took her by the arm. "I need you like the air I breathe." He buried his face in her hair, and it surrounded him. He kissed her with loving tenderness, and when he lifted his face, he said, "There's something you both should know. The dragon inside me is gaining power. I've battled him for months now, barely holding my own. The beast is evil, ruthless. What if I can't stop him?"

Dane walked over to them. "We'll be strong for you."

Lindsey drew him into their embrace. "I know this is hard, Rourke, but there's only one way you can hurt me now, and that's if you leave us. I'm yours. I always will be, but I'm meant to be with Dane, too. I think I would die without either of you. The three of us are destined to be together. I think it's more than just a means to survival."

Dane put a hand on Rourke's shoulder. "I can't live without her. As a Were, I can't function without a mate. I'll turn rogue since we're already bound. It's her or no one. I'll be too dangerous to everyone at the time of the full moon without her. Besides, the wolf pack needs an alpha they can depend on, not some rogue Were. You've seen just a little of what they're up against and what the Were rogues can do."

"I don't get it," Rourke said. "How can you be an alpha, the pack leader, and submit to me? As the leader of all the Lore and a dragon-shifter, I can't share her with you unless you do."

"I guess you answered your own question, Rourke. As leader of all the Lore, everyone submits to you, even the pack leaders." Dane grinned a lopsided smile. "I'm okay with the three of us being together. The real question is will my beast submit? I guess we'll never know 'til we try."

Rourke let out a long sigh and nodded. "Maybe you're right. Wolves are familiar with shows of dominance and submission. You've already shown signs of submission in both your human and wolf forms, so maybe your Were will also recognize the dragon's dominance."

Lindsey touched her fingers to the frown on Dane's forehead. "Weres can be a bit irrational, so when the time comes, know that both of us will be loving you." She soothed Dane with her magical voice.

"Hell, I have a feeling no matter what my Were wants, the dragon-shifter will dominate. I only hope he doesn't accidently toast me in the process."

Rourke grabbed Dane by the shoulders and shook him. "Damn it, Dane, see, that's what I'm afraid of. I don't want the dragon to turn you into a roast, bro." He wrapped an arm around Dane's neck in a fake choke hold and ruffled his hair.

"No one's getting roasted or toasted." Lindsey touched her fingers to Rourke's lips, and Dane laughed.

"Maybe Lindsey can release some of her pent-up charms to get us started. I have a strange feeling she's capable of soothing the savage beasts in both of us."

"Where do we want to start?" Dane wiggled his eyebrows and made Lindsey giggle.

"Let's shift and run. Get some of the tension out of our bodies. I'll meet you back at the hot tub," Lindsey suggested.

Rourke still seemed reluctant. She wrapped her arms around him, and her hair followed suit. A faint mist of silver and gold dust swirled around them, settling over the three of them.

"Whoa, what's that?" Rourke asked.

"Faery dust."

"You're kidding, right?" Dane sounded incredulous and picked some from his shoulder to inspect it. "Like in *Peter Pan*?"

Lindsey burst out laughing and shook her head. "No. Nothing like that."

He sniffed it and then touched it to his tongue. "Whoa, Nelly!" His cock twitched. "Can I fly, too?"

"This dust is the result of a faery's arousal. It has magical sexual properties."

"You're full of surprises." Rourke pulled her against him and nuzzled her neck. The fire shot through her, and the dust sifted over the entire clearing. "Mmm, so you're aroused?" His voice vibrated beneath her skin.

The rumble of desire started in both men right before she shifted and ran.

"I'm always aroused around you. If my special talents can't convince you two a three-way between us is worth the risk, then think about all of us being together forever with faery dust inspiring you every day. That should convince you if nothing else does. Leave it to me."

"She has a good point," Rourke said and patted Dane on the shoulder.

The two males shifted more slowly into their wolf forms and lagged behind for the first part of the journey. She raced them back to the lodge, and when the men caught up, they picked up the pace. The competition grew fierce.

Chapter Nineteen

Lindsey watched both wolves pull up short of the clearing outside her room. Rourke sniffed the air, and Dane shifted back first. She'd never tire of admiring either of them in any form. As wolves, they were powerful and muscular. As men, she'd never get used to touching their glorious male bodies.

After Rourke shifted, he looked around warily as she opened the door. "Come inside, both of you," she suggested.

"She beat you." Dane chuckled in his good-natured way as he stepped inside. "Apparently, Fate knew what she was doing when she bound us to a fae succubus shifter."

Dane slipped an arm around her waist. She nuzzled his chest and gave him a quick kiss before moving closer to Rourke.

He still didn't look any more convinced than he had before about their arrangement, even when she painted herself against his back and circled his waist, allowing her hair to envelope him.

"She had a head start. Besides, I let her win," he argued, but she felt the guarded resistance lift. She ran her hands over his shoulders, working out the tension in his bunched muscles.

"I love the way your mind works almost as much as I enjoy how your male essence makes me feel." She turned in his arms and framed his face with her hands then gently kissed his lips. "If I could, I'd enjoy merging with your soul and Dane's, too. I need you both like the air we breathe, the earth beneath our feet, and the water we immerse ourselves in. I am fae of the elements, I am succubus of the senses, I am a shifter of light, and I am for you."

Rourke stood still as death, not touching her, stiffly withholding a part of himself from her. Without his full cooperation, the three of them could not integrate to complete the whole.

Drawn to Rourke and Dane as if they were a part of her, Lindsey felt an instinctive concern gnawing at her. "Can you understand what I am? My needs, can you accept them?"

"I understand what you are and what you need. I'm sure I can accept them. It's mine I'm not sure about."

"I sense your internal struggle with the decision of how you will proceed with Dane and the final step of our binding. Maybe we should put it off until we're more at ease with each other."

Was he trying to decide if he would go through with it or trying to back out?

"Maybe if we work up to it." He exhaled and cleared his throat. "I'm okay with trying if he is."

Dane moved closer. "Sharing Lindsey will be difficult enough for you to accept, maybe even impossible once the dragon possesses you, yet that whole argument may be moot if it's impossible for you to physically be with me."

Rourke visibly shuddered at Dane's words.

"That can wait. We have a little more time to decide for ourselves," Lindsey said. "By the next full moon, the decision will be made for us."

"So we're in agreement? We're all sure?"

"We want to face our lives as bonded mates with enthusiasm, not dread." She wanted to be clear about the future, because she wanted both men in her life.

"There's another issue," Rourke said. "Wanting to perform and being capable are two separate issues." His voice lowered to a whisper. "You both know I've never thought about being with any man. That Dane is the one makes it more uncomfortable because of my feelings for him."

Lindsey stroked her hand over Rourke's chest and kissed him. "Given enough stimuli and incentive, you will physically claim Dane. Your feelings for him will eventually make it easier." While her tongue teased his mouth, mental images of their three naked bodies, all tangled limbs covered with faerie dust and sweat, filled his mind.

"I guess we'll just have to find a way to deal with it," Dane said with a half grin. "That scene looks too good to pass up. What do you think, Rourke? It's been a while since we shared a woman."

Rourke grunted. "The image Lindsey implanted in my head has my cock rock hard already."

Her mind probed his and reached out to both him and Dane. She sent the ache of desire right behind their balls and watched them sweat. Her power was working on both men.

"What the hell," Rourke said. "I can't walk away from all this."

Neither man could, and neither could she.

"Come here, Dane. Join us. There's no time like the present to get started. Your wolf will accept a submissive role now before you turn fully Were. Rourke's never going to mentally accept this until he's embroiled in the moment, so we may as well try to enjoy ourselves while both of you work your way up to the inevitable."

Dane stepped up alongside her, his heat surrounding her. He cupped her cheek and kissed her with such a tender touch that she was surprised and thrilled. But his arm brushed against Rourke's chest, and everything stopped for an awkward moment. Rourke stepped back and turned away from them.

Lindsey turned in Dane's arms and let him pull the succubus to the surface. His tongue probed her mouth, and his lips brushed hers. God, the man could kiss. "You are very good at that."

She thought of summer days and lazy nights beneath him, surrounded by his scent and filled with his powerful cock. The faery dust glimmered gold and silver on her skin and settled all around the room, coating both men with her need.

Dane chuckled. "I see your faery is aroused. Let's see what we can do for the rest of you."

Rourke growled a low, deep, menacing sound and returned, pulling her out of Dane's embrace and roughly reclaiming her against his chest.

She was surprised to hear a lower growl start deep within Dane's chest, but a firm look from Rourke put it to a quick halt.

Dane glared while Rourke's large hands cupped her breasts and pulled on her nipples. The action shot pure flames of desire straight to her pussy. The way he nibbled at her neck, his warm breath fanning out over her sensitive skin, sent chills up her spine.

Goddess, she didn't know how she'd survive the contrast of sensations running through her body.

****

The fae's desire was obvious with the evidence all around them. But the scent in the air told Rourke the succubus inside Lindsey was working herself to the surface. Her beast was an easy mistress with high expectations. Excitement filled him. He could feel her potential for endless erotic lust like a tangible presence in the room. While Dane stroked her clit, Rourke realized he wanted her so bad his teeth hurt.

When she looked up at Rourke, the iridescent glow to her skin told him she needed him and Dane, too. Part of him was comfortable with knowing the succubus needed more, yet deep down inside, below his alpha wolf, the dragon roared his objection to sharing her. Unless…

Rourke didn't want to face the truth.

The dragon wanted Lindsey, but he would demand Dane first.

His damn fangs brushed past his tongue. Dane and Lindsey turned to him almost at the same moment. Dane licked his lips as his glance touched all the way down Rourke's torso. Rourke's cock twitched with interest, imagining that tongue flicking over it. For a moment, Dane's mouth looked too tempting.

Hell, Rourke couldn't think with Lindsey's pale white skin glowing within Dane's naked embrace.

Rourke's breathing grew more rapid, and his heart pumped harder when he spotted her plump ass cheeks in Dane's hands. They looked so damn delicious he wanted to bite them.

Then Dane turned and flashed his powerful ass. His

muscles flexed beneath his golden skin as he ground against her cleft, and Rourke stopped breathing. He imagined burying his cock between those masculine cheeks.

Shit! The realization hit Rourke like a tank. Something within him wanted Dane, too. He wasn't sure which being was driving this lust, but he needed to touch him.

"Lindsey, come here."

Dane released Lindsey, allowing her to move toward Rourke. He took her in his arms, turning her back to his chest so he could press his hard cock against her sweet ass. He exhaled then bent over her, kissing the pulse at her neck. He hadn't realized he'd been holding his breath while he watched Dane caress her.

He fondled her breasts, rubbing a thumb gently across her nipples until they stood tight and pointed, and then he stopped playing with her breasts and lowered his arms around her waist.

Dane approached and came within arm's reach. "I want to touch her while you do." But he didn't look at Rourke. He just stared into Lindsey's eyes.

Her head fell back on Rourke's shoulder as he drew her more tightly against his hips. Dane ran his hands under her breasts then teased the tips. Her nipples peaked beneath his expert touch.

"Rourke, see how his hands touch me? See how their texture is so different from mine?"

The sight of Dane's hands on her body, arousing her, turned Rourke on. She was right, especially as their mixed pheromones filled the air, and pure lust started driving him.

Dane stepped closer, slowly bringing his body

against hers, pressing his cock against her soft stomach, and took her face in his hands.

"Don't you want to know what his hands feel like on your body?" She mentally sent the sensation of having Dane's hard hands running up and down his arm and the texture of his calloused fingers caressing him.

The knowing smile she gave Dane made Rourke think of angels and heaven. Her visions made him think of sex and sin and damnation.

"Rourke, look at how beautiful his mouth is. Don't you want to taste his lips, feel them traveling over your nipples, down to your cock?"

Dane looked thunderstruck. She sent the impressions like reality through their minds.

"Don't you want this?"

And with that question, Rourke felt the sensation of having Dane's hot mouth suck his cock deep down his throat. God help him, he did want it.

Rourke could barely breathe with the images her mind sent to them. His damn body kept reacting. He heard the rumble as his growl surfaced.

Dane bent and kissed her, a soul-deep kiss, before lifting his gaze. He stared into Rourke's eyes for approval.

Rourke saw the intensity of Dane's desire for Lindsey there in his eyes, but he felt something else.

He heard Dane think, *You know I want this, Rourke. I need you to survive.*

Rourke froze and blocked his mind from Dane, from both of them, and fought back the damn dragon who roared with satisfaction at Rourke's forbidden thoughts.

Damn him, he wanted to taste Dane, wanted to

experience his mouth, and—*oh, hell.* More. All of him. Every fucking inch. Every fucking way.

"He's beautiful, powerful, sensitive." She ran her fingers through Dane's hair and, gaining a handhold, pulled his head toward her mouth. "I love the way your lips taste and how hot your mouth feels on my breasts."

He lowered his lips to her breast and sucked first one then the other as Rourke looked on, his breathing growing more rapid by the minute. His heart thundered against her back.

Dane lifted his head and returned to her lips. He nipped and laved the seam between them before delving inside her mouth, his tongue dancing and tangling erotically with hers.

She kissed him back, dragging him into a drugging kiss. Running her hands over his shoulders, she explored him, knowing what he liked and recognizing his needs. She shared those same images with Rourke, and his hands moved up from Lindsey's waist to her full breasts. His aggression was increasing with his arousal.

He tweaked her nipples while he pressed his hard cock against her ass. "You like this?"

"Oh, that feels so good." Her magic poured out of her into the room and seduced Rourke beyond rational thought.

He ran his hands down her hips and slipped his fingers between her crack. The pressure of his finger against her tiny hole made her heartbeat race.

"I'm going to fuck you here later, and then I'm going to fuck Dane while you watch."

His words forced the fiery heat searing through her pussy to liquefy. Then he leaned over Lindsey's shoulder and pulled Dane's lips against his mouth. The fluid honey poured from her, her erotic scent rising up to encourage the men to stay harder longer. Her succubus was a greedy creature.

Rourke kissed Dane in a dominant, open-mouthed kiss. He paused to demand, "Watch him take my tongue in his mouth." The sound of his deeply aroused voice whispering in her ear sent vibrations through Lindsey's core.

He opened his mouth and devoured Dane's lips again. Both men caressed her as they kissed each other, free to express their feelings for each other for the first time physically. Rourke's dominant tongue-thrusts into Dane's mouth turned her on, and they all understood that Dane accepted them as he would come to accept Rourke's cock penetrating him with breathless, aching desire.

Their mixed thoughts and images filled each other's minds, and Rourke stilled. His eyes filled with apprehension. "Oh, hell, what have you done, Lindsey?"

The dragon eyes crept out from behind Rourke's own, and his skin changed texture and color again. "I can't hold him back."

The eerie voice of the dragon entered their minds. *Imagine us together. You know what I'm going to do to both of you, how I'll fuck you and claim you as mine. Are you ready to submit, alpha wolf? How about you, succubus?*

"I'm not so sure whether my succubus will let you sexually dominate. As she strengthens, she takes sexual control." She wasn't sure what they'd all mean to each other after this night, but she knew this would be good.

They felt too right together for this to be wrong.

As Rourke tongue-fucked Dane's mouth, all of them knew what he expected. Total submission. With that one act, he proclaimed that he would accept his role as master in their ménage. Dane would submit to him. Rourke was the dominant male, the alpha male, and the dragon.

Chapter Twenty

Rourke positioned Lindsey in the middle of the mattress. "I never realized your succubus was going to have a problem with this union, too." His hands traced teasing circles around her darkened nipples.

"It's a control issue, apparently. You're up for the challenge, aren't you?"

For the first time in a long time, Rourke felt that heaviness dragging him down into darkness lighten inside him. The mate for his sexual appetite was waiting inside Lindsey, and Dane would be strong enough to take whatever his darkness dished out.

"Rourke, rub my clit. You know what I need."

"Is that your mistress demanding?" Rourke teased her.

"No, me."

"What's the magic word?"

"You didn't tell me the *magic* word. You told me the word for stop. I don't want you to stop."

"The magic word is... Tell her, Dane. You know it."

Dane leaned over her and whispered the word against her lips. "Please."

She licked his lips before she begged, "Please, someone make me come again. Please. The pressure inside me feels like I'm going to explode."

"Don't worry. When you explode, we'll make sure

it's with pure pleasure."

Dane moved to a position where he could pay close attention to stimulating Lindsey's breasts, nuzzling and licking her hard, erect nipples. He released a wet nipple and nipped the soft skin beneath her ear. She groaned and whimpered as he held her legs sprawled open wide for Rourke's access.

Rourke smiled and knelt between her legs, looking his fill. Her pussy lips glistened with the moisture seeping from her inner core. "See the way her clit protrudes from her labia, all pink and swollen with arousal?"

She lay like a wanton feast before them. She arched her back, and Rourke lifted her hips to take her pussy to his mouth, turning to wink at Dane before he buried his head against her mound. Spreading her legs wider, he went down between Lindsey's legs, sucking her clit and laving her while Dane watched.

"God, she's so wet, Rourke. Give me a taste."

Rourke stuck his fingers deep inside Lindsey and pulled them back out, offering Dane the honey dripping from his hand. Dane licked at Rourke's fingers, sucking them into his mouth. "She's delicious. I've never tasted anything so exotic before." He groaned, and so did Rourke.

"It's my succubus rising." Lindsey barely got the words out between strained breaths.

"Your taste is irresistible." Dane thrust his tongue into her mouth and lightly pinched her nipples. She gasped and squirmed beneath them.

For now, Rourke concentrated on her pussy, licking, nipping, and nuzzling the delicious, plump lips between her thighs until he felt her tension build to a frenzied peak and liquid heat burst into his mouth. "Mmm, you taste like honeyed brandy."

He hummed against her nub and elicited a scream of pure pleasure as more liquid fire poured out of her.

"Rourke, do that again, *please*," she begged.

"Here, let Dane have a taste."

Dane leaned down her body, his long hair skimming her delicate skin, his muscular, golden length draped over her, and he buried his face in her folds, licking at the remnants of her climax.

Her hips collapsed, limp in Rourke's palms. He watched Dane's mouth pleasuring her, and she whimpered as he finished licking her clean. When Dane lifted his head, Rourke leaned into him for a kiss. He sucked Dane's tongue into his mouth and swallowed Lindsey's flavor. "She tastes good on your lips."

"My turn." Lindsey pulled Dane against her, allowing his kiss.

Rourke moved off the bed and grabbed Dane by his hair, pulling him out of his way. Then he smiled, backed up, and leaned down to kiss her himself. Sticking his tongue down her throat, he indicated what he wanted from her, what he would expect from her. He handled his cock. "Now, come over here and suck me."

Dane moved behind her and helped position her on her knees on the floor in front of Rourke. She tilted her chin up. Rourke repositioned his throbbing cock at her lips and waited for her tongue to stroke him. When she opened her mouth and whipped her tongue across the slit, he moaned and pressed himself between her lips. She opened up for him and took his length down her throat. He picked up the rhythm and fucked her mouth, closing his eyes, allowing the pleasure to wash over him.

He wondered if Dane could bring himself to suck him, wondered if he would offer his ass to him in submission or if he'd have to be seduced by the succubus inside Lindsey. The other man's musky scent swirled around him, turning Rourke on instead of putting him off.

He opened his eyes to the sight of Dane on his knees next to Lindsey. Cocking an arched brow at Dane with the obvious matter unspoken, the words came out deep and passionate, hoarse with arousal, when he finally voiced the question. "Are you ready for your turn?"

Dane said nothing but motioned Lindsey aside. He bent over Rourke's cock, and by assuming his submissive position, relieved some of Rourke's concern.

He took Rourke's cock in his mouth, held his hips in his hands and drove the length of his cock down his throat, tonguing the sensitive underside the way only another man would understand. He followed a few deep, quick strokes by licking his balls and sucking them into his mouth and rolling them over his tongue. Dane devoted all his energy to sucking and licking Rourke until his balls rode high and tight and his own hard cock stood mounted between his thighs like a monument.

Once Rourke was satisfied with Dane's submission and the tingling sensation rose up like a snake behind his balls, his cock began to lurch, and he gripped Dane firmly to stop him. He didn't want to come like this, and he'd enjoyed the magic of his tongue almost too much.

They moved back to the bed, and Rourke took the initiative to bend Dane over within reach of Lindsey so he could smell her. But what he really wanted was to watch Lindsey's pussy lips devour Dane's cock while her mouth sucked his own cock to completion.

Rourke encouraged Dane's hips between her thighs, positioning his friend's dick at her opening, rubbing the head in her juices. Dane's knees bent, and his hips flexed as Rourke pushed the flared, mushroomed head into Lindsey's hot, wet slit. Touching Dane's cock felt strangely familiar. He could almost feel the sensation in his own cock when she contracted around Dane's thick shaft. Was it his imagination when he sensed the pleasurable fullness she experienced as Dane filled her and powerfully drove into her white-hot depths? Or was it their connection?

Dane rocked into her, going farther still. Rourke's hands spread her knees wider. She arched up off the bed to take Dane's thick cock deeper inside her, all the way to her womb. Lifting her hips higher, she thrust while he stroked.

She reached up to caress Rourke while arching her hips into Dane's thrust. She seemed insatiable, but no more than they had expected.

"Do you want us both, Lindsey?" Rourke asked.

Her lowered lids barely raised, but she nodded. Rourke straddled her face. She moved one hand out of Dane's hair and took Rourke's cock in her hand and started sucking and licking his long, hard length. She licked his balls then sucked them into her mouth, twirling over them with her tongue before returning and taking him down her throat. Pre-cum bubbled at his tip.

She paused for a breath. "God, you taste good."

The way she said the words convinced Rourke he'd found a woman who really loved sucking cock as much as he enjoyed fucking her mouth.

While Dane fucked Lindsey with a primal energy Rourke felt at his back, she feasted on Rourke's cock like it was her last meal. He pumped in and out, knowing he'd hold out, enjoying the edge of the orgasm for the first time in forever. His climax waited pleasantly just out of his reach, not as desperately as it usually did.

He slipped his cock in and out of her sweet lips with quick, even thrusts as the illusion of the wolf consumed him. He pulled out. She licked her lips and opened her eyes wide. He groaned when he saw they'd glazed into the crystalline, diamond gaze of the succubus, white-hot heat and cold fusion wrapped up in a penetrating, sensual demand. It was then he realized she was going to pull their orgasms from them as nothing before ever had.

He might rule in many things, but in this—how they had sex, what they would do, and how long they could last—well, with her succubus rising, he and Dane wouldn't have much control over the outcome. She was the ruler of orgasms. She could suck their very souls from their bodies if she wasn't careful, so what was another orgasm or two?

Lindsey raked her nails down his chest just as the triggering hitch warned them Dane was about to come. The hot streams of cum shot off inside her while he dragged his extended claws down Rourke's back. She reached deep into Rourke's mind and sent the pain he needed through him. The dragon inside him roared, and she laughed.

The pressure behind Rourke's balls increased with his pace until he couldn't hold back. He howled with the sensation of having her draw the cum from his body like a vacuum, and then she filled his mind with sensations of unbelievable pleasure. He couldn't stop. His climax exploded more powerfully than any he could ever remember. He pumped spurt after spurt into her demanding mouth, and she took it all. This was too good to be true. He hoped their connection would control the dragon when the beast consumed him.

"She's got a tight pussy and a hot mouth. How did we get so lucky?" Dane had rolled to his side, spent for the moment, but not too spent to react to the sound of Rourke's moans of satisfaction as Lindsey's demanding mouth finished stroking him to completion.

Rourke moved back on his knees, lifted her arms over her head, and straddled her breasts. He had to kiss her, taste his cum in her mouth. He cupped her face in his hands and bent down to touch is lips to hers. She opened her mouth and took his tongue inside, sucking it like she had his cock.

He moaned. The taste of his cum in her mouth pleased him, and to his surprise, turned him on all over again. His cock slid between her breasts as he moved down her body, kissing his way past her nipples and the soft underside of each breast, teasing and stroking her belly on his way to her pussy.

He pushed Dane out of the way so he had better access to all of her. She was still sensitive when he touched her clit and very wet when he slipped a finger inside her. All this pleasure from this woman, and she was all theirs, meant for them. It scared him spitless.

"I don't know why, but I'm hard as nails again, and I don't think she's finished with us yet. How you doing over there, Dane?"

"Perfect. This cock works great." Dane rolled to his back and waited, his hands pumping his cock back to erection while Rourke examined every nook and cranny between Lindsey's spread legs.

"I see the blood pumped back into your groin fast enough when you got a look at this." Rourke lifted her knees and pushed his fingers deep into her. He bent over her mound. His mouth engulfed her succulent clit. He licked her nearly to another orgasm before stopping.

"Think about this." Rourke lifted his head to look at Dane's cock, running his tongue over his lips. "I'm sucking your cum from her pussy."

Dane's cock jerked, stood higher, more erect at his words, when Rourke asked, "So, do you enjoy the erotic thought of having me suck you off? Don't get too excited yet. I have something else in mind first."

Before Dane could get too caught up in the image, Rourke flipped Lindsey over onto Dane's chest and positioned her so she straddled his hips with her hot, slick pussy hovering directly over Dane's raging erection. Rourke watched as Dane's hips lifted to enter her, and Rourke pushed her hips down until she had the entire length of Dane's cock inside her.

She let out a soft, satisfied sigh, and Dane groaned. "Fuck, there's nothing like having a hot woman impaled on your rock-hard dick."

"There's nothing like being the one being impaled." She smiled and arched her back, giving both Dane and Rourke the opportunity to admire her breasts.

They were tempting, rounded, and ripe, with large,

pink areolas surrounding darker, pink-tipped nipples. Rourke cupped her full breasts from behind, pinching the pretty, erect nipples gently while Dane's hand steadied her hips.

Dane kept one breast in his hand as Rourke took the other. Then Rourke released her breast to play with her clit. She was wet and swollen. He liked the way she let out little mewling sounds as he tested her readiness. When he heard her suck in short, deep breaths as he circled the nub with his middle finger, he felt empowered. She screamed out his name when he applied just the right amount of pressure.

"God, Lindsey, you know I love it when you come with my name on your lips." Faery dust and pheromones released in the air. "And you smell so damn good." Rourke's voice sounded rough with need. "I need to be inside you, too. You know what I want."

She nodded weakly.

"Are you ready for this?"

"Oh, God, yes," she said.

He bent her forward on Dane's chest, angling her ass up for better access. While Dane took one nipple between his lips and teased it with his tongue, Rourke held her hips in place, struggling for control as his cock jumped. It throbbed with need as he watched Dane's hard, pulsing penis sliding in and out of her bright pink pussy, shiny and wet with her own lubrication. They'd done that to her.

Dane's cock pulled out all the way, and she cried out at the loss. Still outside her, Rourke jacked Dane's cock once or twice. Then he stuck his fingers into Lindsey's tight opening, scissoring her wider. Pulling some of the dripping juice, he wiped it all over his shaft until it glistened, and then he wiped more over Dane's cock and her pussy lips. He tested her entrance with three fingers, then four. She was tight, but they'd fit.

Rourke took Dane's dick in hand, gripped it firmly against his own, and then re-entered her with both cocks, stuffing her full of cock.

Lindsey cried out as they filled her.

"Does that hurt?"

"Oh. No. It. Is. Wonderful. More. Deeper. Ohhh."

"Geezuz, Rourke, what the hell has she done? I love the way this feels. Your damn dick is so fucking hard pressed up against mine like this."

"Yeah, this is good," Rourke admitted, and he closed his eyes as they thrust, cock-to-cock, as one inside her.

The faery dust mixed with their perspiration turned into glittering diamond crystals that disappeared on touch. Lindsey's moans came faster, and Rourke had one more opening he wanted to penetrate before they finished with her this time.

"If you think this is good, darlin', wait 'til I fill you here." Rourke pulled out of her pussy and placed the tip of his dick against her back entrance. "What do you think?"

"I think your pleasure is mine."

"Good answer."

She was plenty wet. Liquid heat poured out around the base of Dane's cock. Rourke rubbed the natural lube over his shaft and tested her entrance with a finger, then two, and gently stretched her before pressing his cockhead against the tiny hole. His crown entered her opening and disappear inside the tight ring. He rocked in slowly, gaining ground each time.

Her breath hitched.

"Okay?" he asked.

"Yes...yes. Don't stop."

"You're so fucking tight I can't believe it." He could feel how full she was with Dane still inside her pussy.

"Whoa," Dane moaned, and his eyes rolled back in his head as Rourke's cock finally, fully penetrated her. Once Rourke's entire shaft was buried to the hilt inside her body, he could feel the ridge of Dane's dick pulsing in and out of her.

Rourke started the pace and let Dane adjust. He pumped into her tight opening, feeling the completion of being inside her while Dane filled her pussy. He didn't think he'd ever experienced anything as good as the feel of Dane's cock gliding against his inside her together, but this, feeling this tight slide through the common wall while her anal ring gripped him so tight, was even better. He thought the sensation alone would pull the orgasm from him this time. He didn't think he'd need the pain or the fear. It was like nothing he'd ever experienced. Unbelievably, the act of sharing her this way, bringing her so much pleasure, brought him more pleasure than he'd ever conceived was possible.

He forced himself to unblock his feelings and opened his mind to her and Dane, revealing his own pleasure through their mind link. He felt all the fantastic sensations she felt and the pleasure Dane was experiencing. It had to be because of the psychic bond they'd formed. The phenomenon made the sexual experience more complete, totally fulfilling. The connection between them swirled around them, in them, and through them.

Rourke couldn't hold back the pressure building behind his balls any longer. Her powerful sexual essence poured into his soul. His climax erupted, and her body milked him with her own orgasm, forcing both men to spill their seed. Rourke's followed just a moment after Dane's last stroke exploded inside her gorgeous, blonde pussy.

****

"Come on, Rourke, let's shower," she said, pulling Dane with her.

"In a minute."

Dane followed Lindsey into the bathroom to clean up while Rourke sat on the edge of the bed with his head in his hands. The sound of the water running made his damn cock twitch. He should be in the shower with them, but he wasn't sure he could finish this thing despite how far they'd come. It was easy enough to get caught up in the moment, but he still feared the damn dragon inside him. The monster wanted flesh and blood.

He heard Dane chuckle, and Lindsey giggled. He wanted to be part of that.

What the hell.

When he opened the door, they were already soaped up and locked in a passionate embrace. Engrossed in their kiss and plastered in each other's arms, Rourke realized he still had mixed feelings about sharing. He wouldn't allow those feelings to ruin the moment or engulf him in petty emotions as he watched Dane kiss her and touch her.

Rourke closed his eyes to sort through his feelings. Instead of jealousy, he was surprised to feel only arousal. Her succubus nature mesmerized him, and her scent intoxicated him. He stepped in and joined them. He lathered up, and they helped him. Having their hands all over him and her scent in the air had his cock rocking at full staff.

"God, you smell good." He bent to kiss the pulse at the base of her neck, needing to sniff at the blood flowing beneath her delicate skin. "Mmm."

Just smelling her scent fill the air would be more than enough to have the men's cocks ready, engorged, and throbbing. But she was so erotic in her need, so beautiful in full arousal, that it almost hurt to look at her. She shimmered. The light and heat she gave off wrapped the men in her pleasure.

"You're so beautiful, so perfect," Rourke murmured against her neck.

Dane stepped in closer to her body, cupping her face in his hands, and kissed her. "You taste so good, too." He moved his knee between her thighs, sandwiching her between the two men. Dane's chest brushed against the backs of Rourke's hands as Rourke cupped her breasts. He dropped his hands to her waist and slid them farther down her belly to her mound.

He unintentionally brushed Dane's cock. It pulsed eagerly in reaction to the contact, but Dane didn't move away or into Rourke's hand.

Dane held his ground, and so did Rourke. Neither man breathed for a long moment, and then Rourke turned his hand. Dane leaned into his palm, and Rourke closed his fist around Dane's cock. He could appreciate the texture as he explored without the urgent need he felt when his fist gripped his own. Dane's cock lengthened and turned harder beneath his touch. Caressing a cock other than his felt similar, but the velvety-soft skin covering Dane's hard interior felt different in Rourke's new point of view. He kind of liked it.

Rourke caressed Dane's cock with one hand and strummed Lindsey's clit like a banjo until both were panting fast and wild with need.

"Rourke, please, you both feel so good against my body, but I need more. Let's go back to bed. I want you to take me in your mouth and eat me like dessert while Dane fucks my mouth."

"No, maybe next time. It's time to finish this, Lindsey. Make it happen."

As the desperate sound of her voice begged him to devour her, he felt the beast within him urge him to take what she offered—take it all. He wanted to fuck Dane while his face was buried between Lindsey's wet folds, he wanted Dane on his hands and knees before him in submission, begging to be fucked. *No!*

He turned off the water and stepped out of the shower. He tossed two towels at Dane and took one for himself. "Dry her off."

He wasn't sure who wanted to do all those things. *Maybe it is me.* But the beast within him sure as hell did, and if he didn't find a way to merge himself with the dragon, he'd lose every shred of control and humanity left to him.

Between the irresistible scent of Lindsey's shiny, dripping pussy calling to him and the idea of fucking Dane's virgin ass, Rourke could hardly hold himself in check. "Are you ready for this?"

Dane answered with a low, husky voice. "I don't know."

"Then get ready." Rourke purposely reached down

and cupped Dane's balls, rubbing them and stroking his friend's erect dick with the knowledge only another man has. "How about now?"

Dane leaned into Rourke's touch as if unable to resist the sensation. He groaned a deep, throaty sound of pleasure when Rourke stroked his hand up and over the flared head, taking his time at the opening. When a pearled drop of liquid escaped, Rourke spread the moisture over the mushroomed dome and teased the sensitive entrance.

It was going to happen. She was making this all possible with her gift.

****

Rourke kept reminding himself that men had never sexually appealed to him. He'd never imagined the prospect of touching or being touched by a man, but touching Dane and having Dane's hands and mouth on him felt good.

Fucking him? Rourke stilled.

A part of him experienced a rush at the thought. Although the heightened arousal he suddenly felt at this prospect felt foreign to him, sticking his dick in Dane's tight, virgin asshole and claiming him as part of their ménage seemed right. He couldn't wait to be buried inside him, pressed to the hilt, rocking that old rhythm and returning the pleasure as Dane's virgin canal gripped his cock like a man's tight fist.

Watching Dane as he bent over between Lindsey's thighs and burrowed his tongue into her pretty, pink cleft turned him on, especially when he drew a moan of immense feminine pleasure to her lips.

"Jeez, Rourke, look at this. She's pink and petaled like a flower, and look at this pretty bud." Dane touched her nub, teasing, and she groaned.

"It's so sensitive from your attentions I could come just rubbing my thighs together."

"Then let's get this show on the road. I'm ready for some more succubus attention. Let me see how much faery dust we can raise." Dane tickled her breast with his tongue and made her giggle.

Rourke thought it was the sexiest sound he'd ever heard. Then Dane chuckled and lifted his muscled ass to Rourke in silent invitation. *Fuck, that was sexy, too.*

Rourke took a deep breath and ran his hands between Dane's butt cheeks, spreading them. He lowered his head, bent, and licked Dane's asshole to lubricate him, cupping his balls while he did. He stroked Dane's cock and pumped it, bringing him to full erection while he fingerfucked his ass until a needy groan replaced Dane's rapid breathing.

"She tastes delicious, and that feels so fucking good. Damn, touch my balls again, Rourke. They're aching."

Dane's cock hardened beneath Rourke's hand in anticipation. His own cock was stiff with hope. He refocused his efforts on Dane's cock and balls, rubbing his hand up and over the sensitive tip, stroking until a pearlescent drop of liquid seeped from the opening, and then he returned to lightly squeeze the ache from Dane's balls.

Both he and Dane groaned.

Suddenly, Rourke imagined a pleasure he'd never considered. His cock started twitching with impatience as he rimmed Dane's rear opening with his tongue, preparing to penetrate him. Rourke desperately needed to slide between Dane's muscled cheeks and into the dark depths of his tight entrance.

He lubed his fingers with the cream dripping from Lindsey's pussy and tested Dane's opening, scissoring two fingers inside him. "How does this feel?"

"God, it feels fantastic." Dane groaned. "You don't know what you're missing."

"I've heard that somewhere before. Sounds like a conspiracy." Rourke teased Dane back because he needed to slow down. Despite wanting the immediate sensation of the tight, hot grip on his cock, he would do his best to hold back the dragon and give Dane time to adjust to his size before he buried himself up to his balls.

He penetrated the opening with the tip of his dick, stroking, stretching, and slowly pushing in until he was fully seated inside him with his balls pressed firmly against Dane's perineum. As well-endowed as Rourke was, Dane took every inch of his cock before Rourke started the steady beat he knew would drive them all over the edge.

Dane grabbed Rourke's hand, stopping him before either of them reached orgasm. When he lifted his mouth from Lindsey's swollen clit, he noticed how her legs trembled in anticipation.

With Rourke still buried balls deep in Dane, both men paused to focus on the gleaming, pink petals surrounding Lindsey's swollen nub, pink and chubby and delectable as any strawberry.

"Geez, will you just look at that?" Dane's cock jumped in Rourke's hand at the sight of Lindsey's thick, golden honey seeping from her slit and spilling out as faery dust glittered their skin. "Have you ever seen such a beautiful sight?"

"You make my golden honey, you make my faery dust, and you make me beautiful."

Dane carefully lifted himself up on his knees, and kneeling before her entrance, he leaned into her kiss.

"I want you inside me so deep we are one," she murmured.

"Who could resist a request like that?" He slid farther up her body, kissing her breasts and then her lips more thoroughly this time. He moved slowly, slipping his cock between her thighs while Rourke stayed firmly entrenched in his ass.

She touched Dane's chest and ran her hands over his tight male nipples. "Can I taste them?"

"Later. I can't take much more and hold on." Dane took both of her breasts in his hands and simultaneously tweaked her nipples, rolling and tugging them before his lips lavished attention first on one, then on the other. He parted her folds with his fingers, preparing to penetrate her. He lowered his head over her lips and kissed her as he slid his cock into her creamy, hot opening.

She took Dane's full length inside her, and Rourke felt her pleasure as Dane filled her.

"Rourke, she feels so good gripping my cock like this. Come on. I'm not going to last long."

He pumped a long, hard stroke into Dane's ass and then picked up the rhythm, driving Dane harder and higher within her. He sensed Dane's strain from holding his imminent orgasm in check.

Images poured through Rourke's mind. There was more between Dane and him than what they'd once believed. Something told him they belonged together, somehow always had. They'd nursed at the same woman's breast. Being of one mind, sharing their bodies with each other and another woman, the woman they both cared so deeply for, suddenly didn't seem strange anymore. The emotion he felt for Dane was his, but the sexual drive belonged to another part of him, a part lying dormant until Lindsey released it.

He palmed Dane's balls, knowing how the sensation felt, and smiled when he heard the man's responsive moan of pleasure.

He merged with Dane and experienced the slide of his body along Lindsey's and the allure of her scent. With his shaft penetrating Dane's ass and his mind participating in all their sensations, the tension mounting in his groin built to unbelievable proportions.

Lindsey stared up at both of them, her magic swirling quicksilver in her eyes. Instead of holding back, Rourke drove harder, fucking Dane into her, giving them both all the pleasure he could, and opened his mind to them, enabling them all to share their feelings during this moment with one another.

"Rourke! I feel connected to you," Lindsey said. "To you, too, Dane. To all of our essences. I am for you."

"We are for you," the men vowed in unison, the two sounding almost like a chorus of deep voices.

Rourke reached between his legs and started rubbing Dane's balls against his own, rolling the nuts inside gently as he began his rhythm, stroking in and not quite out. When he released them, their balls lightly slapped together as Dane lifted his ass for more and pressed his balls back for the full effect.

Rourke gasped then shouted "Damn!" when he heard Lindsey whimper with desperation beneath Dane.

His cock hardened more than he'd ever experienced inside Dane. The pleasurable sensations gripped him. He loved how all of it felt so erotic, so wonderful.

When Rourke pressed deeper inside Dane, his hands gripping his hips, Dane slowed his pace. Rourke sensed the pressure building in his balls. His own cock ached with need, and he pressed his cock deeper. "Good?"

"Fuck. Good. Fuck me harder," Dane responded through loud breaths.

"Harder?"

Then the first rumble came, a low growl, emerging from deep within Rourke's chest.

"Good!"

"Damn, your ass feels so tight." Rourke fucked Dane with a hard, pounding thrust, the kind of force he held back with Lindsey. Yet all the while he fucked Dane, he focused on Lindsey's face.

Dane kneaded Lindsey's breasts and explored her mouth with his tongue before Rourke heard him groan with satisfaction.

Dane's cock filled Lindsey then he suddenly picked up the pace, riding her hard to his climax. Rourke merged with Dane and experienced the slide of his body along hers and the allure of her scent. With Rourke's cock being squeezed inside Dane while he endured all their sensations, the tension mounting in his groin built to unbelievable proportions. He smelled Dane's blood, and his fangs elongated. His eyes rolled back in his head, and he bit into Dane's jugular, sucking down the thick, rich blood.

Dane yelled out Lindsey's name and bit her. Sucking her blood at her breast while pumping his orgasm into her, he collapsed, spent. Her incisors elongated, and she drove them into the other side of Dane's throat. She drank from him until Rourke reached around Dane and gently pinched her clit. She opened her mouth and released Dane's throat. She screamed Dane's name and climaxed.

Still, Rourke waited and didn't release the dragon.

He'd pulled out when Dane had collapsed on Lindsey, and Rourke shoved him to the side to keep them both from crushing her. Dane was weak from blood loss, and Lindsey was spent. He shook Dane, but there was no response.

"Listen, Dane, this is important. You have to take my blood while I'm inside you. The dragon is a danger to you until we've completed the blood exchange. Dammit, can you hear me?"

When he didn't respond, Rourke asked, "Lindsey, can you bring him around?"

"I'll try. What's wrong?"

"We took too much of his blood. Now the dragon is rising in me, and I'm not sure I can hold it back without you both."

Lindsey rallied to Rourke's fear. "He has to take your blood, and we have to complete the ménage bond now. We can't wait."

Dane moaned as Rourke rolled him to his back and spread his thighs for better access. She licked his cock, bringing him back to erection.

"Can you rouse his beast?" Rourke asked.

Dane was barely conscious from the blood loss. The scent of fear and danger filled the room. They couldn't wait much longer.

Lindsey shifted into her wolf and rubbed herself

over Dane's body, leaving her scent everywhere on him. Dane's canines extended into long enough fangs to get the job done, but he was too weak to move.

"Lindsey, come here and start the blood flow from my jugular," Rourke said.

The white wolf nuzzled Rourke affectionately. "It's okay, Lindsey, you won't hurt me."

He lifted and separated Dane's knees and placed his cock at his entrance. "I'm going to fuck you, Dane, while you take my blood, or you won't survive. The dragon wants to kill you. You can't let him. Do you hear me? Do it, Lindsey, now."

She bit down on Rourke's throat from behind and backed away to let the blood flow freely. The metallic scent of blood filled the room as he thrust into Dane and leaned down, embracing Dane and pulling his mouth to his neck. "Drink, Dane. You are for me."

Within a few seconds, Dane lapped with more strength, pulling the blood and power from Rourke as he thrust to complete their bond.

Lindsey returned to her succubus form and offered up her wrist to Rourke while he held back his beast. He accepted her offer.

His cock burned, and his sight went crimson with the bloodlust as his dragon tried to raise the violent demon, but Lindsey's blood held him back. Her blood tasted of spring and cherries and wine. Even though the pressure in his balls demanded release, Rourke was afraid to let go.

Lindsey stroked his body, pinching his nipples, licking, scratching, and nipping down his body. She squeezed his ass as he hand-pumped Dane's cock and drove his own cock into Dane with a strong, steady rhythm.

"We can't keep this up for long." Rourke knew he had to come soon, "Or the beast will overpower us all.

"Let me help." Lindsey ran her fingers up inside her pussy until her hand dripped with her lube. "I hope you like this." She licked his scrotum and cupped his balls.

He groaned. "What's not to like?"

Then she gently pushed a lubricated finger into Rourke's tiny, puckered opening.

"This." She pushed past the sphincter and pressed firmly against the magic spot that sent his cum spurting into Dane in wave after wave of power, and he bellowed a mighty roar in the process. Dane's cock jerked in Rourke's hand and exploded almost simultaneously. Cum shot all over his chest.

Dane gasped through shortened breaths. "Is it over? Is the connection complete?"

"I think so," Rourke said, easing his cock out of Dane. But the horror of knowing there was an entity inside him who'd wanted to kill Dane pissed him off.

"From the satisfied smiles, I guess you both loved it," Lindsey said, sweeping her hair over her shoulder.

"I felt everything you experienced." Rourke grinned at her.

Blood dripped from all their faces.

"Since we all took so much of each other's blood," Dane said, "we may also have exchanged abilities."

"I'm pretty sure we're all infected with the Were virus, but since we're bound, that won't be an issue," Lindsey said and rolled to her side.

"Now all we have to discover is if I picked up your dragon or demon DNA from our little tryst." Dane ran his hand up Lindsey's back as she stroked his calf.

"I'm going to head outside. I feel a little strange," Rourke said.

Both Lindsey and Dane stopped dead.

"Are you all right?" she asked.

When he didn't answer, she and Dane jumped to their feet and followed him. They watched as Rourke shifted into the wolf.

"Why is the hair on the back of my neck standing on end? He doesn't look right."

"He's infected with your Were virus," she said.

"I guess this answers one of your questions," Dane said.

"Rourke," Lindsey said, "the Were virus has affected your wolf."

"It's freaky. It looks like you, your wolf, and something else are in there."

"You should know, bro. This is what you become when you turn. At least we're bound to Lindsey. We won't turn rogue."

"My cousin Macalister is a leopard-shifter, and she's in a ménage relationship with two shifters. One's a wolf, and one's a mountain lion. Her partners own Fantasy Lodge. While they were helping her go through her first shift, the Were-cat accidently drew blood, so now they all turn Were at the time of the seasonal full moons."

"Do you think there's a reason we've all been infected by the Were virus?" Dane asked. "When I checked our blood, I thought the Were virus reminded me of the demon DNA attached to the dragon DNA in Rourke's blood. Is there a connection?"

"The virus first appeared when the portal between

the Underworld and the Otherworld opened. When demons started stealing and impregnating the shifter females, the Were virus spread."

"That verifies the identifiers in my DNA. From what I've been able to figure, some of Rourke's mitochondrial DNA is wolf-shifter. His Y-chromosome makeup is more complicated. I wonder why our three-way connection is needed to complete the bond."

"I'm feeling a little more in control." Rourke shifted into his human form and went back inside. "You should have plenty of time to research your theories."

"Hell, it's a good thing you shifted outside, or your head would be through the ceiling." Dane said. "Hey, how about we all hit the showers, then head to the hot tub for a soak? I'm feeling my succubus rising."

"Dane, you crackpot, I told you males are incubi." Lindsey gave him a gentle shove.

"Sorry, I forgot. My *incubi* is rising, and it needs you to take it in your luscious mouth—"

****

Toweling off after the shower, Rourke finished first then ran his fingers through his hair and pulled on his pants. "Put on some clothes, Dane. There's a lot we need to settle, and I feel better talking business with pants on. You, too, Lindsey. Especially you." He tossed her a bath towel, and when she wrapped it around her body, he said, "That's not really better."

Dane pulled on his jeans. "If we're going to fight Aryan one day, we'll need all the information and help we can get. Our wolves won't be enough, and the Weres are unstable rogues unless they're bound."

"My dragon's reaction could have been even worse because of my demon blood."

"Now, when Beltane comes," Dane said, "we'll be strong enough in any form to withstand the shift, and we can build our defenses against a future attack. I'll gather the shifters and see what I can do with the Weres."

"If Aryan decides to return, it won't be until after the vernal equinox," Lindsey said.

"Good," Rourke said. "It'll give us plenty of time to test out our different forms, especially our succubae, incubi, whatever."

"You still have to go to the Council and tell them you've accepted your position on the Council."

"What position?" both men chorused.

"Did I forget to mention I confirmed Dane's bloodline is royal? He is the dark prince, the one we've been awaiting, the wolf-shifters' leader. Once I realized we were all destined for one another, I checked with the forest fae. Dane, your mother truly was the reigning alpha female, and her father was the prince when she ran from her pack to be with your human father."

Dane grinned like he'd won the lottery. "I knew I was meant to be king."

"Now who's got the big head? And uh, she said *prince*."

"Semantics."

Celia shimmered into the room in all of her sparkling splendor. The men didn't even blink.

Lindsey waved a hand. "My aunt, er, the Fae Princess Celia, Seer of the High Council, and a royal pain in my a—"

"Uh, uh, uh. Don't say something you'll be sorry about. You sounded awfully happy a few minutes ago. All that 'harder, more, oh, oh, oh—' "

Lindsey's face heated. "Celia, you didn't!"

"No, I didn't. I just guessed. Now say you're sorry."

"Humph, I'm sorry."

"Now, down to business. The other seat left open on the Council is the Leader's seat. It's waiting for one with dragon-shifter blood, but the Council Leader must be part of a ménage so there is no possibility of instability." She glared at Rourke. "They've been waiting over thirty years to fill your position. Do you accept your responsibility as Leader of the Lore, dragon-shifter?"

Rourke looked at Dane and Lindsey. "Can we move our operations here to Colorado, Dane? Maybe to Dragon Mountain?"

"I don't know why not."

"Yes, Celia. *We* accept the position as Leader of the Lore."

He reached out both hands to Dane and Lindsey. When they touched, a blinding light sealed their bond.

"Excellent. I propose a triple celebration—a wedding, a coronation, and a birthday party for you three next full moon." Celia poofed and was gone. *"Oh, please don't forget we must present them in fae."*

"What?" Rourke asked.

Lindsey shook her head. She removed her towel slowly. "First one to the hot tub gets to kiss me first." Then she poofed out of the room, leaving the towel behind to drift to the floor.

Dane and Rourke just looked at each other, and Rourke growled. "I'm not poofing under any conditions."

"I'm not poofing, either. I'm the damn prince."

With that, both men scrambled to the door, tripping over each other.

"I'm going to punish her for this," Rourke said.

Dane pushed him out of the way. "I'm going to help."

"Come and get me. My faery dust needs kissing off."

The sound of two men groaning in defeat filled the night air. Then a young woman's giggles could be heard, and then, finally, sighs.

E.L. March

About the Author

E.L. March (author Eliza March) focuses on the reader's senses with her breathless award-winning romance stories. She loves writing about sunny days filled with flowers and butterflies, and stormy nights immersed in candle-lit bubble baths, listening to haunting music, and drinking Champagne. Reviews claim her characters are three dimensional and her plots uniquely fascinating.

Eliza is living her own romance story with her fated love and her happily ever after.

~*~

Visit E.L. at

www.ElizaMarch.com

~*~

To chat with E.L. March and other Wild Rose Press authors of erotic romance, join us at

www.groups.yahoo.com/group/thewilderroses.

The Lion, the Leopard, and the Wolf

Enchanted Mountain

By E.L. March

Macalister Cameron's fantasy comes to life when she's snowbound in Fantasy Lodge with two incredible men vying for her attention.

"What if your romantic fantasy became possible? Two gorgeous hunks, one dark and surly, the other blond and bright, lived to please and fulfill you? What if you burned with passion and only these two alpha males could satisfy you? What if you found out they had a dangerous secret, and it included you?"

Also Available
from The Wild Rose Press, Inc.
and major retailers.
Lady and the Pack
Line of Lilith Book Two
By R.A. Boyd

Kayla Taylor isn't looking for a relationship. She's used to her quiet bubble of school, work, and staying far away from her dysfunctional parents. But landing her dream job with the local werewolf pack brings on a new murderous world of crazy that makes her relationship with her parents look like a walk in the park.

Pack member Patrick Belman tells Kayla she has a new boyfriend, and he's it. In the midst of their happily ever after Kayla discovers a civil war among the wolves that has been brewing since the Garden of Eden, and her undiscovered lineage is the final prize. Kayla is pulled into the world of the wolves by the bonds of love and family, something she had longed for since her childhood.

But sometimes, she just wants her nice little bubble back.

Thank you for purchasing
this publication of The Wild Rose Press, Inc.

For questions or more
information contact us at
info@thewildrosepress.com.

The Wild Rose Press, Inc.
www.thewildrosepress.com

Two Alphas...one succubus...
a legend born or denied...

"Game, set, match," Rourke announced. The sexual tension seemed to lessen in the presence of the pines. This place drew him in and soothed him. He desperately needed a peaceful place.

"You sure that wasn't out?" Dane always pushed the limits.

"In by a foot."

"Out by…" The banter died on Dane's lips.

"Was not," Rourke started to argue at Dane's hedge, but he didn't miss his brother's distraction. He immediately looked over at him.

The familiar cocky smile, the one Dane thought looked sexy and he reserved for only the hottest women, quirked a corner of his mouth. Rourke considered teasing him, goading him into another argument, until he followed his brother's gaze in the direction of his interest.

The scene slowed down in Rourke's mind, playing out in slow motion. Air blew out of his lungs like he'd been gut-punched, and his insides twisted into knots at the vision drawing Dane's undaunted attention. No wonder his brother looked thunder-struck.

The blonde from last night.

The sight of the woman standing on the veranda was enough to suck rational thought from any man's brain. Not only was she perhaps the most beautiful thing he'd ever seen, but sexuality exuded from her like heat from a bonfire.

As desirable as a *succubus*.